Liberty Letters™

The personal correspondence of
Hannah Brown and Sarah Smith

The Underground Railroad, 1858

Nancy LeSourd

Zonderkidz

Zonderkidz®

The children's group of Zondervan

www.zonderkidz.com

Liberty Letters, The Personal Correspondence of Hannah Brown and Sarah Smith
Copyright © 2003 by Nancy Oliver LeSourd

Map, from THE UNDERGROUND RAILROAD by Raymond Bial. Copyright © 1995 by Raymond Bial. Adapted and reprinted by permission of Houghton Mifflin Company. All Rights reserved.

This book is a work of fiction. References to real people, events, establishments, organizations, or locales are intended only to provide a sense of authenticity, and are used fictitiously. All other characters, and all incidents and dialogue, are drawn from the author's imagination and are not to be construed as real.

The wheat contest and pig calling incident are composite sketches attibutable to the *Virginia Sentinel,* WPA interviews, and stories of Asa Moore Janney.

Requests for information should be addressed to:
Grand Rapids, Michigan 49530

ISBN: 0-310-70350-6

application made for CIP

Liberty Letters is a trademark of Nancy Oliver LeSourd.

Produced in association with the brand development agency of Evergreen Ideas, Inc. on behalf of Nancy LeSourd. For more information on Nancy LeSourd or the Liberty Letters series, visit www.Zonderkidz.com/libertyletters.

Editor: Gwen Ellis
Cover design: Michelle Lenger
Interior design: Tracey Moran
Photo layout design: Merit Alderink and Susan Ambs

Printed in the United States of America

03 04 05 06 07 /❖DC/ 10 9 8 7 6 5 4 3 2 1

Goose Creek, Virginia

Third Month 17, 1857

Dear Sarah,

You have been on my mind constantly. I miss you so much. When will you and your family be able to visit us here at Goose Creek? I hope you will have occasion to visit this summer, for it has been much too long since we have been together—more than a year since we have seen each other. When Grandfather goes to Philadelphia to buy plantings for his nursery, I pester him to take me with him. Yet Mother and Father say I must stay in school and not be traipsing all over creation.

Sarah, you know me well. You know that my mind and heart are somehow bigger than Goose Creek, Virginia. I yearn to see the world. At least Grandfather lets me see most of Loudoun County. I have been helping him on his latest surveying project. He is updating his map of the Snickersville Turnpike and often takes me along to make notations. He and Joshua hold the chain and the compass while I carefully take notes of the measurements they call out, in Grandfather's surveyor's notebook. Ever since he published his map of Loudoun County—the one he did with your uncle four years ago— he has more mapmaking business than he can manage.

Remember when I last wrote about Joshua? He has become invaluable to both Uncle Richard and Grandfather. He works at the foundry most days. But whenever he can, Grandfather spirits Joshua away to help with the surveying. Grandfather says no one else holds a surveyor's chain as straight and tight as Joshua does. So you see, Sarah, it is rather convenient, don't you think, that I should go along to assist Grandfather with the note taking? Joshua makes me laugh. And he is rather handsome. I am glad he came to our village. He has no mother or father. Yet everyone here likes him so well. It is as if the entire village has adopted him. He has impressed Uncle Richard with his diligent work and quick mind. Grandfather enjoys his sense of humor as much as his chain-holding skills.

Speaking of Grandfather, I think he is most happy when he is on a towpath or road in his buggy with his viameter, measuring, calculating, plotting, and planning. He loves to be free. I think I am just like him.

Do ask your parents when you might come to Goose Creek. Many here ask about you. I wish you still boarded at Springdale School next door to Evergreen Farm. Then we could be together every day. I miss rushing home from school to visit with you. We had such glorious times.

Affectionately,

Hannah

Goose Creek, Virginia

Third Month 26, 1857

Dear Sarah,

What an amazing sight! About one hour before sundown, Grandfather, Mother and Father, my younger brother David, and I gathered at the top of a nearby hill facing west. The almanac said there would be a full eclipse of the sun, but I was unprepared for anything so incredible. Imagine the sun being completely covered by the moon. A strange and wondrous sight indeed—although we were warned not to look directly at the sun. Doing so could burn our eyes and blind us.

Grandfather says God has many wonderful things to show us if we are watching. He says the trick is to remember that God's surprises far outweigh anything we can possibly imagine. Something to ponder, don't you think, my dear friend?

Your sun-and-moon-and-stars-watching friend,

Hannah

Philadelphia, Pennsylvania

Fourth Month 9, 1857

Dearest Hannah,

I miss you, too! I also miss Springdale, Goose Creek, trips to Purcell's Store in your grandfather's buggy, and even young Israel, who teased me mercilessly. Is Friend Eliza Janney still teaching at Springdale? She taught about what matters in life: liberty for one and all.

Do you remember when she came from New York to teach at Springdale? There was much consternation in Leesburg that this northern-bred woman was teaching children antislavery ways. Of course, what did they expect from someone teaching at a Quaker school?

Is Principal Janney still traveling as much as ever? He has such a heart for sharing his wisdom at the Quaker meetings in the country. His writings are well received here.

How is your grandfather? Uncle Robert looks forward to their visits together. He often comments on what a fine mapmaker Friend Yardley Taylor is. You must share all your stories of your adventures with him.

Do tell me all that is going on there in Goose Creek.

Your devoted friend,

Sarah

Goose Creek, Virginia

Fourth Month 15, 1857

Dear Sarah,

I received your good letter and will report to you all the Springdale news I have heard. Your beloved teacher, Friend Eliza Janney, has been spending much time taking care of her husband, Friend John. Do you remember that she married Principal Janney's son? He has taken ill with a severe cough and nothing done for him seems to help. The doctor frequently attends to him. His family often takes him to the springs in hopes that he will recover. You may wish to write Eliza, for she would be encouraged to know how she has influenced your life.

Today Grandfather, Joshua, and I spent the entire day in the buggy. We measured, remeasured, calculated, and laughed and laughed. It was an absolutely perfect day. The weather was glorious. It was exhilarating to be out in the clean spring air. As usual, I kept the notebook and carefully wrote down everything Grandfather called out to me as he and Joshua worked the chain and compass. Mathematics is not my favorite subject at school. Joshua and Grandfather can make calculations in their heads faster than I can write them down.

Joshua says he loves to spend time with Grandfather, because he is so talented. I have never thought of Grandfather that way. I know he enjoys many things. He enjoys his job delivering the mail from house to house. He enjoys his surveying and mapmaking. He enjoys plantings and tending his nursery with some of the most exotic plants one can imagine. Most of all, though, he enjoys his family. I always feel so loved when I am in his company. He does not think me dull or silly or childish. When I am with him, I feel as if I could do and be anything I wish. I think it is the same for Joshua.

Joshua has had many disadvantages. One would never know it, though, as he is so friendly and kind. He speaks of his future rather than the past. He talks with Grandfather about planting, mapmaking, surveying, working at the foundry, and inventing. He is excited about working with Uncle Richard on a new project—a special plow that will make tilling the soil much easier.

With every good thought toward you,

Hannah

Philadelphia, Pennsylvania

Fifth Month 21, 1857

Dearest Hannah,

What a delight to read your letter! Oh, I do miss our times together. We had such fun. Father says that you are welcome to visit anytime. Ask your grandfather again if you might come with him. I have much to tell you.

Father, Mother, and I have been busy with our many activities and with making sure our packages are delivered safely. It is more dangerous now to be in the delivery business. Ask your grandfather to explain. I should close for now.

Your friend,

Sarah

Goose Creek, Virginia

Sixth Month 2, 1857

Dear Sarah,

I asked Grandfather about your delivery business. It sounds quite mysterious. I was confused when I read your letter. I showed it to Grandfather this afternoon when we were in the buggy. After glancing at Joshua, who was rolling up the surveying chain, Grandfather whispered to me that we would speak about it later. He said I was not to say a word about this to anyone. On the way home, Joshua tried to make me laugh, but my mind was preoccupied.

This evening Grandfather asked me to come to the barn with him to brush down his horse, Frank. You remember Frank, don't you? He is such a solid horse, deserving of such a solid name. Frank suits him, don't you think? Anyway, Grandfather explained that there is a system called the Underground Railroad. He said it helps runaway slaves go from place to place until they reach freedom. He said many from our faith are involved.

Grandfather explained that it used to be a simple matter to help slaves escape across the Potomac River just 14 miles from here. They would take a short passage through the state of Maryland into your state of Pennsylvania, where they are free. But since the Fugitive Slave Act in 1850, slaves are not safe until they reach Canada. Grandfather also said that anyone caught helping a runaway slave escape can be jailed. Then he brushed away some of the hay in Frank's stall and showed me a trapdoor.

Grandfather did not say a word. He just let me look inside with my lamp. I saw a bed of straw and a blanket. I stared inside for a long time. Then Grandfather lowered the trapdoor and spread the hay over it again. Frank nuzzled me, but I could not move. Things were whirring around in my head so fast, I thought I would faint. Grandfather put his hands on my shoulders and said, "The Lord said he came to proclaim liberty to the captives—to set free those in bondage. How can we do any less?"

We walked back to the house in silence. Then I lit my candle stub and came straight to my room to write this letter. Sarah, is your family involved? Are you part of this Underground Railroad? Are you in danger? Are we in danger? How long has Grandfather been hiding slaves right here at Evergreen Farm? I have so many questions. I cannot sleep. So I am posting this letter the first thing in the morning. Since Grandfather is the United States Postal Service mailman, I won't have to go far.

Your friend forever,

Hannah

Philadelphia, Pennsylvania

Sixth Month 14, 1857

Dear Hannah,

I showed Mother your letter. She says we must not speak of such things by letter, especially by any letter posted in Virginia. She has a plan, however. Your grandfather arrives tomorrow. I will send back with him a special present for you. I am so sorry he will not let you come with him this time. Mother says that we will soon be together, but much needs to be done here. Mother and I attended sewing circle again this week. I have worked my fingers to the bone with sewing. The need for clothing increases. I will explain more later. Hannah, I am afraid that our friendship quilt must wait a bit longer. There is not time right now to work on it.

Have you seen Joshua lately?

Your devoted friend,

Sarah

Goose Creek, Virginia

Sixth Month 25, 1857

Dear Sarah,

Your mother is so clever! No sooner had Grandfather arrived from Philadelphia than I inquired about my present from you. He smiled and handed me a little seedling in a clay pot. After a few moments he laughed loudly and said, "Hannah, you should see your face! It is all scrunched up trying to figure out the mystery of the seedling. Come with me." Then Grandfather led me to a table in the greenhouse and turned the pot upside down. All the dirt not attached to the roots rolled out onto the table, as did a small leather pouch. Inside were your letters!

What a magnificent idea your mother had to hide your letters in a pot, since Grandfather goes often to Philadelphia for his plantings. When I write back, Grandfather will carry my letters to you in a pot with cuttings from Evergreen that he is selling in Philadelphia. No one will ever guess our secret. From time to time, Sarah, we should send our regular letters in the United States mail, but if we must speak about things better left unspoken, this will do quite nicely.

Grandfather is full of stories of his time with your family. I only wish he had taken me with him.

Tonight Grandfather had a surprise for me. He had taken some of our best cuttings with him to Philadelphia to sell. There was one cutting from our ginkgo tree for which he found an interested buyer. The buyer did not have enough cash to purchase our cutting, but he did have with him a velvet pouch of pearls and other gems. Grandfather selected a perfect, luminescent white pearl in payment. Tonight he gave me the pearl. He said that when he saw it, he thought of my purity of heart and wanted me to have this as a token of his love for me.

Have you worked on our friendship quilt lately? I will take my leather pouch to bed tonight and read your letters by candlelight.

Affectionately,

Hannah

Philadelphia, Pennsylvania

Sixth Month 21, 1857

Dear Hannah,

By now you have my letters in hand. Were you surprised? Mother thought of the plan and your grandfather approved. Father said that means we should expect to see more of your grandfather. I pressed them all to let you come as well, but your grandfather said your schooling comes first. I think he is weakening, though, because later I overheard him talking with Father. You may be able to accompany him on a trip to Philadelphia when he brings his latest map to be published.

One night Robert Purvis from the Antislavery Vigilance Committee arrived to speak with Father and your grandfather about a package that was delivered here for our care—a slave from Maryland who escaped two weeks ago. Father told your grandfather about how the Underground Railroad is operating and that it is so much more dangerous now to help slaves to freedom. I overheard them discussing bringing even more slaves across the Potomac, as time is short for such activities.

Your grandfather spoke of patrols with dogs trained to track slaves. He said that for several months now they have been coming by Evergreen routinely. Mister Purvis encouraged him to continue his efforts, because now more than ever the Railroad must operate quickly and carefully. The last thing I heard was when he told your grandfather that his skill in mapmaking was given to him by God for the assistance of those in bondage. I know you have often said that your grandfather knows every road, path, canal, and creek in Loudoun County. Perhaps that is why he is so good at helping slaves in their run to freedom.

Hannah, you must consider these things. Your grandfather may need your help. Now that he has shown you the hiding place, you have a special responsibility to ask God what he would have you do with this knowledge. When your grandfather showed you the straw bed, did you not think of the comfort of your own bed with its pillow? When your grandfather showed you the blanket just big enough to cover the straw bed, did you not think of your own ample covers and warm fire inside? Can you turn away from those God brings to your door at Evergreen? Hannah, I hope I have not offended you. But you have a good heart and you must think about what I have said.

Always your devoted friend,

Sarah

Philadelphia, Pennsylvania

Sixth Month 22, 1857

Dear Hannah,

I have only moments to dash off this letter to you. Your grandfather is stopping by this morning for my little pot. I only want to quickly tell you that no matter what you decide, I am forever your friend. I am sorry if my words in my last letter caused you any distress. I know that it is much easier for me here in a free state to speak of such things. You live in the largest slave state in the country, and you must be very careful. I understand that. I know you have had little exposure to the harshness of the southern slave trade. Your Quaker village of Goose Creek is a haven of liberty in a state filled with slave owners. As Quakers, we do not purchase people to do our bidding. You are very blessed not to know firsthand about the cruelty of the peculiar institution of slavery.

On the other hand, I have heard too many stories told by fugitive slaves who have come to our home. It grieves me that men can treat other men, women, even children as they do. God made each of us in his image, and we should cherish one another. I have cried many tears as runaways have spoken of the cruelty and pain they have suffered. The last slave here from Maryland was obedient to his master despite whippings no human should endure. He reached his limit when the master sold his wife and his child to a plantation down south. He pleaded with his master to let him go, too, but his master would hear none of it. That night he ran away and did not look back. He hopes to go to Canada, where he can work and make money to purchase his wife and child, but he does not even know to whom they were sold.

It is a horrible business, this buying and selling of humans. It is a most horrible business.

I feel deeply, Hannah, and ask that you understand my passionate pleas for you to join us in helping others. You and I are from different sides of this United States, though our states almost touch one another. There is a line between slave and free that every slave knows only too well. Although we are on different sides of this Union, we are both on the side of the good Lord. He will guide you, Hannah.

Devotedly,

Sarah

Goose Creek, Virginia

Seventh Month 22, 1857

Dear Sarah,

Grandfather and I worked in the garden today and readied the soil for the plantings. Grandfather is quite pleased with the bald cypress tree he bought in Philadelphia. He says it will be given a place of honor right near the underground stream so it can have all the long drinks of water it needs to make it through the summer. Sarah, Grandfather said he tried to convince your father to journey to Virginia next month, but your father said it was more needful for Grandfather to come north to Philadelphia and bring special packages. I thought he was speaking of our packages and our secret mailing system, but instead he was speaking of the Underground Railroad and the need for Grandfather to bring slaves to freedom.

Thank you for understanding my uncertainty at this time about all this Railroad business. Until last month I had no knowledge my family was involved at all, much less here at Evergreen. I have this terrible feeling I keep trying to push way down inside. I'm afraid things are going to change.

Your friend,

Hannah

Goose Creek, Virginia

Seventh Month 25, 1857

Dear Sarah,

I rushed home from Oakdale School today. Grandfather and I are at work on a mapping project. Mother and Father have determined that I may help Grandfather all he needs as long as my schoolwork doesn't suffer.

My brother, David, is getting older now and can help with the animals and the garden when I am out with Grandfather. Uncle Oliver is working in the plant nursery this summer. That means it will be just Grandfather and me on many days. Oh, how I love to be with him. Whether we are in the garden or on the road in the buggy, we are happy. I think Grandfather is glad that I am with him.

I have not seen much of Joshua. He is working long hours with Uncle Richard on the plow. I think Grandfather misses him. I am not as funny as Joshua. Mother is requiring me to work on my handwork this summer. I wish you had time for the friendship quilt, as I have absolutely no interest in the other stitchery I am supposed to do.

We had a grand picnic on the Meeting House grounds. The children played and the food was plentiful. My cousin Carrie Taylor asked me to tell you hello. She misses your company, as well. At the meeting there was a loud argument among the men. I overheard one of them tell Grandfather that he needs to be more cautious about what he is printing in the newspaper. Grandfather drew himself up to his full height and replied that if a man doesn't want to read truth in the newspaper, then he should use it to wrap fish.

Mother explained to me that Grandfather had written the *Sentinel* a letter, which was not only published here but also reprinted in the *New York Evening Post.* The letter only increased the anger in some people over his position on the Fugitive Slave Act. Grandfather believes there is a higher law he must follow, and if he is willing to accept the penalty—which could even be jail—then he should continue to follow his convictions. I am concerned that Grandfather is becoming too outspoken about his antislavery views in these perilous times.

Your very worried friend,

Hannah

Goose Creek, Virginia

Seventh Month 27, 1857

Dear, dear friend, Sarah,

All I have feared has come upon us. Grandfather's life *is* in danger. I walked to the store today and waited for Joshua at the corner near Oakdale School. Joshua was late. Finally I gave up on him and started walking to the store. Then I saw it. Sarah, posted on a tree was a notice that attacked Grandfather for his position on abolition. It was horrible. In big letters at the top it said, "TO YARDLEY TAYLOR: CHIEF OF THE ABOLITIONIST CLAN IN LOUDOUN" There it was, for everyone to read.

Listen to how this person described Grandfather!

"Now look straight down the road leading to Goose Creek—ten to one you will see, emerging from the wood at the end of the lane, a square-built, heavyset, huge-footed, not very courtly figure of an old man, mounted on the vertebra of a somewhat lusty animal, with one hand tightly grasping the rein, and the other hanging on to a little black bag containing the Goose Creek mail."

Sarah, I could read no further. I was furious. Who was this person calling Grandfather a huge-footed man? Why, my Grandfather is the strongest man I know. The writer even called Frank names! What kind of person begins a letter attacking both man and beast because of the manner in which God has created them?

My hands were shaking as I continued to read:

"You declared your innocence of the charge upon which you were arrested and brought to trial—the charge of aiding in the escape of a fugitive slave. But when subjected to the test of a searching examination, you admitted that a runaway slave came to your house. I note it seems rather interesting that all the runaways seem to stumble across your residence. Of course, it is all accidental. You knew him to be a runaway slave, yet you took him in, fed him, and sent him on his way to Pennsylvania rejoicing. And what was your excuse for this offense? That you were acting in conformity with the principles of your faith. This is monstrous! Monstrous!"

Sarah, the broadside notice told of other attempts Grandfather had made to help slaves escape. It said that Grandfather had been arrested before and had faced a trial at that time. I know nothing of this. It must be a mistake. Then, in the middle of this notice, I read:

"You possess no small amount of skill in the business of putting slaves through, and others have a right to expect the superior skill and ability with which you have heretofore managed the affairs of the Underground Railroad Company. The immediate vicinity of your residence is entirely favorable to the furtherance of your designs. Soon, however, that will come to an end."

I ripped the notice from the tree and ran all the way home. Mother and Father were in the parlor with Grandfather. I showed them the broadside notice. I grew impatient. Sarah, it seemed as if it took an eternity for them to read it all the way through twice—very carefully.

I could not stand the silence any longer. "Grandfather, is this true?" His silence told me what I needed to know. I pleaded, "this Underground Railroad business is too dangerous. What if you are arrested and imprisoned again? Let someone else help the runaways get to Pennsylvania." But Grandfather would hear nothing of it. He believes that God has put him down right here at Evergreen precisely because the house is aptly positioned to assist runaways. Sarah, I know Evergreen is close to the river and helpful to the slaves, but it is still our home. How can Grandfather risk his life and ours?

Mother and Father wanted me to calm down and go on to the store. Joshua would be worried, they said, and we should continue on as if nothing has happened. After all, they said, the foolishness of those who would publish their opinions on a tree rather than in the company of the faithful should be ignored. Grandfather would not let me go, however, without asking me that question again. The conversation was no different than before. He is just like you, Sarah, wanting me to get involved in this Railroad business. "Hannah," he said, "you must decide. You are old enough to help me, but you must decide."

I told him again I do not want to help. The awful sinking feeling I felt when I pulled that broadside down from the tree overcame me. I pleaded with him more fervently than ever before. "Grandfather, I just want things to be the way they were before the slaves started to come to Evergreen—just you and me and the garden. I don't want to hide slaves or help them across the river. I don't want to sacrifice our reputations or maybe even our lives."

Grandfather just stood at the window for the longest time as he looked out on our garden filled with boxwood, lilacs, roses, poppies, peonies, and lilies, many of which he had bought on his trips to Philadelphia. Then he sighed deeply and said, "Things will never be the same again. Times are changing, Hannah. You can sit by and watch it all happen or you can be part of it. You must search your heart and decide what *you* should do. Will you help me get the slaves to freedom? It is just a dozen miles from our home to the river. Sheriffs and bounty hunters are watching those last miles carefully. I am going to need more help this year than last. Your mother and father and I have discussed it. They have granted their permission for you to help me, but it must be your decision."

They were all looking at me. I could not answer, so I ran out of the room. Sarah, I feel so ashamed. The whole family is so enthusiastic about this plan—everyone but me, that is. What is the sense of bringing trouble into our home? I simply must come to Philadelphia soon to talk with you about this.

Your distressed friend, who is very unenthusiastic
about this whole business,

Hannah

Goose Creek, Virginia

Eighth Month 22, 1857

Dearest Sarah,

What a wonderful time we had together! I was so glad Grandfather took me with him to Philadelphia to meet with your Uncle Robert Smith. I never knew there was so much involved in publishing a map. Grandfather's map of Loudoun County continues to sell very well, and I am so proud of him. We discussed the latest map project and Mister Smith is enthusiastic about publishing it.

I enjoyed meeting your Aunt Alice. She is a devoted Christian woman who was so gracious to me while Grandfather and your uncle conducted their business. She said, "I sense you do not have peace in your heart." I hope I did not seem rude, but I could not tell her what troubles me so.

I miss you, Sarah Elizabeth Smith!

Affectionately,

Hannah

Goose Creek, Virginia

Ninth Month 28, 1857

Dearest Sarah,

A new school year has begun. This year I am to study much more difficult mathematics and computations. Perhaps I will be of even more assistance to Grandfather. You inquired as to the state of things since the posting of the broadside. I must unburden my heart to you, though I am uncertain when I will be able to get these letters to you. Grandfather is not planning to go to Philadelphia anytime soon, and Mother says I must not speak of these things—especially in writing, especially now. So I will keep this bundle of letters for you until he travels to Philadelphia again. Perhaps after wheat harvest.

Sarah, you must understand that I can no longer pretend these goings on of Grandfather do not cause me great distress. Mother wants me to pretend as if nothing were wrong. Pretend as if nothing were wrong? When Grandfather's name and crime of abolition activity is posted on trees in every corner of our community? These postings constitute a challenge to our family, yet we remain silent. I cannot understand this at all.

Why is it that freeing slaves is more important than defending ourselves to those who would call our character into question? Others say Grandfather has committed treason, and anyone—*anyone,* Sarah—who assists him in his abolitionist activities is as guilty as he. Yet Mother and Father are willing for me to help this year in these "activities." Whatever can they be thinking?

At the meeting on First Day after the broadside was posted, no one spoke of the notice or its contents. Everyone acted as if all were well. Friend Samuel Sonns quite enthusiastically greeted Grandfather, almost as if he approved! Joshua told me I appeared troubled, and asked if he could help. It was very nice of him, Sarah, but then he must never know what I have been asked to do. I am so confused, Sarah. Mother says that although Joshua has become a good friend to the family and a valued apprentice to Uncle Richard, he is not to know about the slaves staying at Evergreen. I suppose that no matter what the broadside says, it is only one person's opinion.

I remain your humble but very confused friend,

Hannah

Philadelphia, Pennsylvania

Eleventh Month 10, 1857

Dear Hannah,

It has been ages since a letter has arrived from you, so I eagerly opened the ones that arrived today—in a rather large pot. When I saw that the pouch was stuffed full, I knew much was on your mind. I read your letters over and over. I am so sorry you are troubled. Remember what the Lord said: "Let not your heart be troubled, neither let it be afraid." Have faith in God, Hannah. He will guide you by his Spirit.

There is much activity here. We have had one fugitive slave after another in our home. It seems as if the sounds of distant trumpets call them, urging them on, now more than ever. Already there is much talk about what this Union has become and whether it can stay together. We are working with the committee to do all we can to raise money for the cause. Next month, the week before Christmas, the Philadelphia Antislavery Society is putting on its annual bazaar. Mother and I are working tirelessly to make goods to be sold. My sewing circle meets three times a week now. The need for clothing is great. You can't imagine how tattered some of the runaways' clothing is, and they must dress warmly for Canada. I am so sorry that I have not been able to sew my square for the friendship quilt. I do hope you will understand. It was good to see your grandfather again.

Affectionately,

Sarah

Goose Creek, Virginia

Twelfth Month 3, 1857

Dear Sarah,

I have a solution! I know a way for us to correspond more often and work on our quilt at the same time. It came to me when I read your last letter. We can slip our letters inside a quilting square. It would appear to be ordinary needlework, but we can place our letters between the calico and the backing and slip-stitch it closed. Then we will be able to write whenever we want and post them in the mail. And now you will *have* to work on our friendship quilt!

Your friend,

Hannah

Philadelphia, Pennsylvania

Twelfth Month 23, 1857

Dear Hannah,

You, my dear friend, are as clever as your grandfather and as bright as he says you are, despite the fact that you do not like school. You just have too much adventure in your soul, Hannah Brown. Enclosed is my first square for our quilt.

Our bazaar was a glorious success. We had wonderful speakers, including Robert Purvis and Thomas Garrett. Friend Lucretia Mott was there, too. Her commitment is inspiring. We raised much-needed funds for the antislavery movement—some $17,000 this year. Hannah, there are some who travel in the South appearing to be slave owners. They purchase slaves to set them on their way on the Underground Railroad. Often the slaves who are purchased are wives or children of those who have already escaped. Sadly, the southern planters have learned to raise the price substantially if they learn of such an attempt. A slave who would otherwise sell down the river for $500 to $1,000 will often have a price of three times that much.

I miss you so.

Forever your friend,

—Sarah

Goose Creek, Virginia

Third Month 4, 1858

Dear Sarah,

I have not written to you in such a long time. My school-work has been keeping me busy, and Mother has determined that I must improve my stitchery. I am just no good at things a woman should know. I much prefer the outdoors, the garden, or surveying with Grandfather. But Mother says I am fifteen now and will soon be ready for marriage. I must concentrate on these necessities of a woman's life.

Thus yesterday was another day of lessons in womanly things. I have never minded milking the cows in the early morning, but the steady pounding and repetition of making butter in the churn is so tiresome. What the cow gives in minutes takes hours of churning. Best to just drink the milk, I say. My mind wanders as I churn. I think of the adventures I might have had if I had been born a boy. I would want to grow up to be just like Grandfather—except that I would not want any part of that Railroad business.

Today was baking day. Early this morning I was sent next door to Springdale School for some fire, as ours went out overnight. Today we made eight loaves of bread and four pies. We have some dried apples and peaches from last summer, and those should be delicious when mixed with honey. Alas, Sarah, it was a disaster. Mother directed me in preparing the bread mix. When I added the hops, however, I mixed it right into the scalding milk. Mother cried out, as our hops supply is fairly low. I had killed the yeast. Right then and there. When the mixture cooled, I fed it to the pigs with their mush. Curious, I asked Mother if we could bake a loaf of the mixture so I could understand what happened to the hops. Frankly, I didn't see the difference between warm milk and hot milk in regard to causing bread dough to rise. Mother, with a wink at Father, approved the experiment. I think Mother is just like her father, my dear Grandfather, Yardley Taylor, for she knows a girl will not fully learn a thing unless she learns it with her hands as much as with her mind.

That loaf was in the oven for hours, yet it never rose. It cooked, all right, but when I broke it open, it was as dense as a brick. Mother got a good laugh out of our baking day and remarked that perhaps we should try again next week. I sighed, knowing that my lessons in wifeliness need much work. Grandfather, however, took a big hunk of my loaf of killed-yeast bread, chewed a very long time, and said heartily, "Well done!" The entire family laughed, as I looked puzzled trying to figure out if Grandfather meant I had done the job well or that my bread loaf was well done!

Your very undomestic friend,

Hannah

Goose Creek, Virginia

Third Month 8, 1858

Dearest Sarah,

I must write you posthaste. Your dear friend and teacher, Eliza Janney, met with great sorrow yesterday. Her husband, John, could not be restored to health and died in their home. Mother told me that up until the end, John trusted in the faithfulness of the Lord to see him through this shadow. It is reported that when Doctor Daniel Janney arrived, he asked Friend John if he were passing through the valley of the shadow of death. Friend John answered, "Oh yes, yes! He is merciful." Your dear friend never left her husband's side, and at the end he whispered his prayer heavenward in hushed tones that she had to lean near to hear: "My Savior, take me to yourself." Then he closed his eyes and passed on to heaven.

It is a puzzlement to me, Sarah, how someone so near death can speak words so full of life. Could it be that when one has walked with God, at the end of life it seems as if one is just going over a hill? We here watch until we think one is no more and has vanished from our sight. But is it possible that such a one has just walked to the top of the ridge and is now over the hill, beyond our view?

I must post this right away, as it is mail day here in the village and I want you to know right away so you can comfort your friend and good teacher.

With mercy and prayers,

Hannah

Goose Creek, Virginia

Third Month 29, 1858

Dear Sarah,

I went with Grandfather to Waterford in the wagon today. We bought hominy, soap, and the drawing paper Grandfather needs for his maps. It was good to see our friends at noonday. Grandfather and Friend Isaac Steer spoke quietly. I was very curious to know what they were talking about, but I could not hear. So I thought I would catch up on all the news of Waterford from Sarah Steer and the Dutton girls, Mollie and Lida. By the way, Mollie says she remembers you fondly from your time at Springdale.

They told me about the growing concern of the Friends in Waterford over the nation's impending crisis due to slavery. Sarah Steer sounds a lot like Grandfather. Why can't we just leave this situation alone? Fortunately, no packages have arrived at Evergreen since Grandfather first told me about it. I like it this way. Nice and quiet.

On the way home Grandfather stopped in Leesburg. We visited Dr. Moore. Grandfather spoke with Dr. Moore for a long time while I studied his apothecary. I am so glad I have not been sick in more than a year, for if these medicines taste as horrid as they look, I should be loath to take them.

It will soon be planting season, and everyone is working to ready the fields. We will plant corn, wheat, buckwheat, and rye. After the harvest last season, the land was prepared with plaster and lime and should yield an outstanding crop this year if the weather permits.

I look forward to working in the garden with Grandfather. I speak of nothing else all winter. Grandfather tells me I am much too impatient. Grandfather has always loved winter. He says it is the season of rest. Rest for land, perhaps, but not for Grandfather. That is when he works on his maps. Funny, though, Sarah, as much as Grandfather loves winter and the beauty of the snow, lately he can talk of little else but spring. He seems impatient for the snow to melt and the buds to burst forth on the bushes and trees. He knows that soon afterward will come the runners—those slaves whose only desire is to cross the Potomac River to freedom in your state. They will come, Sarah, as they have more and more each year. They will come to Evergreen and to our home. They will come and bring danger to our family.

With fear and trembling,

Hannah

Goose Creek, Virginia

Fifth Month 14, 1858

Dear Sarah,

Master William Smith has let me take home *Gummere's Treatise on Surveying*. I am so happy. I will study it all summer. If churning butter, making bread and pies, and stitchery calm my mind, then the surveying text will excite it again. Grandfather just smiles when he sees me pouring over the calculations and drawings in the text. I know they are somewhat advanced for my mathematics skills, but I will master them in time.

No visitors. No packages. Lots of patrols, though. Dogs barking late at night, patrolling Goose Creek. Often they come by Evergreen, as if the sheriffs believe we are harboring a fugitive. I am glad there has been no reason to be afraid of such an accusation. At night Grandfather often stands at the window lit by a candle and sighs. I know he wishes a fugitive would find his way to Evergreen. Not me, though, dear Sarah. Not me.

Your friend,

Hannah

Goose Creek, Virginia

Sixth Month 18, 1858

Dear Sarah,

Today as usual I walked to the corncrib and gathered an armload of corn. I began to call for the hogs. "P-o-o-o-e. P-o-o-o-e. P-o-o-o-e." The hogs were rooting around in the leaves on the ground for food, but when they heard me, they poked their noses up in the air, sniffed, and then came tearing down the hill. Their snorting and squealing filled the air. Three of them galloped down the hill so fast, they began to bump against each other. I laughed so hard that it caught me off balance and one of those hogs knocked me down. The corn flew up in the air and scattered on the ground around me. I brushed myself off and rubbed my poor bruised leg, but I could not stop laughing. I came into the house, sore and bruised but still laughing. Mother tried to act concerned, but Father could not contain himself. He had tears streaming down his face from the laughter. They had seen the whole thing from the window.

See what you are missing in your city life?

Your forever farm friend,

Hannah

Philadelphia, Pennsylvania

Seventh Month 4, 1858

Dear Hannah,

Your pigs have gotten the better of you, dear friend. Perhaps you should ask your father for farming lessons to go with your cooking lessons? You did not say if Joshua was around to witness your feeding methods!

I must thank you for telling me so promptly about dear Friend Eliza Janney's loss. I wrote her immediately upon learning the news of her husband's passing. She wrote back to say my words had comforted her.

If there is one thing I have learned from the business our family has engaged in these past few years, it is that life and liberty are very precious.

Your forever city friend,

Sarah

Goose Creek, Virginia

Seventh Month 15, 1858

Dear Sarah,

Joshua helped me pick berries today. We found plenty of dewberries and gooseberries and carried home several pailfuls. This was one time I was glad I have mastered the art of making a pie, as Joshua stayed until it was finished. I poured him a tall mug of milk to go with his pie fresh from the oven. He said he had never had such a delicious treat. I think he stretches the truth, dear Sarah, but I was surprised at how proud I felt at his compliment.

While he ate the pie, we spoke of surveying. Joshua is much quicker than I in mathematics and he has studied algebra. He explained some things that had been confusing in *Gummere's Treatise on Surveying*. He is a good teacher, Sarah, and we share so many of the same interests. He never speaks of slavery—for or against. I have no idea where he stands on this issue. Of course, I do not ask either.

I surprised myself at my boldness when I asked Joshua, "What does it feel like to be an orphan?"

He responded, "Hannah, dear Hannah, what does it feel like to have loving parents?" Seeing my confusion, he continued, "For me it is all I have known. Just as for you the love of your mother and father is all you have known. But because we both trust in the Lord, one way of living is not better than the other."

I said, "I am sorry, Joshua, but I am not sure I understand you."

He explained, "Hannah, the true happiness of orphan children comes from knowing that when their parents forsook them, the Lord began watching over them. I have always experienced God's care in all my affairs. He has led me and continues to show me his fatherly care even though my mother and father are dead. You have experienced the tender mercies of God in the form of a beloved mother and father. Don't we have the same thing to rejoice about—the way God has watched over us, for me directly and for you through your parents? Yet both of us experience God directing and guiding our lives."

Sarah, I wish I had the confidence Joshua does that God is directing my life. I feel as though one day slides into the next, with the same tasks and chores before me. I know that my training is for a domestic life, with a husband and children, that will likely be mine one day in the future. But my mind is eager to explore and learn those things typically reserved for boys. I do know this, however: Father and Mother love me dearly and pray for me every day. I am sure that one day this will all be sorted out. But for now I find myself a bit envious of Joshua's certainty of his faith in God and God's plan for his life. Joshua reminds me of you. You are so sure of the calling of God in your life and God's call of your family toward this Railroad business. I, however, am conflicted and confused by it all.

I am just glad that this year has passed without incident. Grandfather says it is because of the increase of patrols around our village and our home since the posting of the broadside. Father says it is because this route is becoming too dangerous and more slaves are going westward over the mountains to the north. Mother says it is not time yet and that just as the land remains fallow before its most important crop, sometimes the home must rest before its most significant guest may arrive. I think it is because I pray so very hard each night that no slave will find his way to Evergreen.

Your faithful friend,

Hannah

Goose Creek, Virginia

Eighth Month 23, 1858

Dear Sarah,

Joshua is frequently at Evergreen these days, helping Grandfather and Father cut and stack hay. In a few weeks the harvest of the wheat will begin and we will break from school. I expect to see more of Joshua then, as we will prepare the lunch meal for the harvesters each day. I suppose those cooking lessons of Mother's are not so useless after all.

Your friend,

Hannah

Philadelphia, Pennsylvania

Ninth Month 2, 1858

Dear Hannah,

With this square, our friendship quilt is progressing nicely! Your stitchery is much improved, despite your lack of interest in such things. You speak much of Joshua lately. I must visit you and meet this young man who seems to have captured the attention of my good friend.

Devotedly,

Sarah

Goose Creek, Virginia

Ninth Month 15, 1858

Dear Sarah,

The wheat harvest has begun. Now, I know that you and your mother go to the store to buy the wheat flour to make your bread. Here in Goose Creek we harvest the grain that is ground into the wheat flour that finds its way to the store shelves. There is much excitement about this year's harvest. Not only has the weather been perfect this summer, but also the crop has come in strong and stands tall. There should be plenty for our needs and enough left over to sell or exchange. Thus we may have a few luxuries we otherwise might not be able to afford. School is out for two weeks, as everyone is needed for harvesting the wheat crop.

Joshua is cradling wheat with the men. He challenged my Uncle Richard and Uncle Oliver and Father to a contest. He believes that at the end of the day he will have cradled more wheat than any other man. As all want to get the wheat in as quickly as possible, they took Joshua up on his challenge. David ran back to the house to tell Mother and me as we were preparing the lunch. Mother smiled and said

Joshua will have his hands full with Father in the match. No man cradles wheat as fast as Father. I felt torn. Of course I want Father to win, but then, Sarah, it also would be good if Joshua won.

When we went to the fields at ten this morning to take the lunch, the men were in good spirits. The children carefully placed each man's shocks of wheat in a pile with his name. We had made a delectable meal with cool springwater for the men. They were very appreciative but took only moments to eat their food and then hurried back to the work of cradling the wheat.

The men did not stop their work until nightfall. The next morning they bound the cuttings into sheaves, and the children carried the sheaves to the threshing floor. The children stacked the sheaves in piles, again according to the man who had cut them. At the end of the day, the men gathered to determine the winner. The total amount of harvested wheat came to 120 bushels! Word went out in the village and by nightfall many had come to see if it was true—that we had harvested 120 bushels of wheat. There was much merriment among the men, and Father, who shocked the most wheat, teased Joshua, who came in second, by saying age and experience sometimes win out over youth and enthusiasm. I can tell Father likes Joshua, Sarah. I think I do, too.

Your affectionate friend,

Hannah

Goose Creek, Virginia

Tenth Month 16, 1858

Dear Sarah,

Pumpkins, pumpkins, pumpkins. That is all I have to say. Due to the good climate this summer, we have more pumpkins than ever before. I suppose I know what kind of pies we will be making this Sixth Day.

Joshua and I worked with Grandfather and Father to pick a bounteous supply of apples today. Some we will dry and store for winter. All the others will be left for Mother and me to convert into pies, butters, and sauces. Tomorrow we will take a wagonload of apples to the cider press. Oh, I do hope the cider stays sweet for a longer time this year. It is so delicious.

Your friend,

Hannah

Goose Creek, Virginia

Eleventh Month 5, 1858

Dear Sarah,

It is cold enough to kill the hogs now. Rather nasty business that I prefer to stay out of, but Mother insists that this year I must learn to make hogshead cheese. Oh, this constant training by Mother in these domestic ways is never-ending! Joshua came to help Father slaughter the hogs. They are preparing the hams for smoking in the smokehouse now. This is not the time to speak with Joshua. I prefer him with a surveyor's compass or a mathematics book—rather than covered in hogs' blood.

Always your friend,

Hannah

Philadelphia, Pennsylvania

Twelfth Month 15, 1858

Dear Hannah,

We are hard at work here preparing for the antislavery fair to be held the week before Christmas. This will be the largest bazaar ever, and we are determined to collect as many items as possible.

Aunt Alice has been working with me for a month on what are sure to be the most treasured items at the bazaar. Aunt Alice appreciates the finest of fabrics and has in her possession some of the most beautiful silk textiles I have ever seen. She gave me several of her beautiful dresses to cut up for sewing. Together we have sewn six silk purses out of each of her dresses. We have sewn every stitch as perfectly as possible. The purses are made of light blue silk, lined with cream silk, with silk drawstrings. On the front of each purse, we stamped the fabric with a transfer print of an enslaved man in front of a slave shack, with a young child on one knee and another child in his arms. In the background is a church steeple and another slave plowing a field.

Since we are selling such wondrous things this year, we have made a list of the items to whet the appetite of those who would purchase the goods for gifts. We have fine stationery, paintings, jewelry, and embroidery. This year we even have some unusual items from those in Europe who stand with us. There is Parisian notepaper stamped with initials, as well as perfume, sandalwood fans, and statues. We should bring in more contributions this year than ever before.

Devotedly,

Sarah

Goose Creek, Virginia

Christmas Day, First Day, 1858

Dear Sarah,

On this day that celebrates our Savior's birth, I want to wish you the very best. Thank you for being my friend. Today our meeting was glorious. Many Friends were moved by the Spirit to share of their love of God and deep appreciation for the gift of his Son's birth.

Your friend,

Hannah

Philadelphia, Pennsylvania

Twelfth Month 31, 1858

Dearest Hannah,

 Our antislavery fair was a huge success. We made more money than ever before. I am sorry I haven't been able to work on our friendship quilt until now. Today I worked a nice square for you with some leftover silk from the purses we made. Aunt Alice tells me you are worth the finest silk found on earth, though I know you dress in calico. Aunt Alice says she is praying for you. I have not told her of your questions and confusion nor of the decisions you must make, but somehow she knows. She has always had a great deal of spiritual insight. She asked me to tell you that the light within you will guide you when you need to know the way. She also asked me to pass along this letter from her.

Forever your faithful friend,

Sarah

Philadelphia, Pennsylvania

Twelfth Month 31, 1858

Dear Hannah,

I sense we are kindred spirits. When I was young like you, I also yearned for a safe path—one that would protect my happy childhood. I shared a special closeness with my father that delighted me, and I wanted nothing that might disturb it. It was much the same as your friendship with your grandfather. Yet when difficulties come—and in this life they do—it could be that they will prove your confidence in the Lord as never before. Trust him now for everything, and see if he does not do for you exceeding abundantly more than you could ever ask or think. He will do this for you, dear Hannah, not according to your power or talents but according to his mighty power. Watch and see. You may well encounter a situation in which there seems to be no way out. Trust the Lord, Hannah, and he will show you the way. This life of faith is lived moment by moment in absolute trust.

Affectionately,

Alice Smith

Goose Creek, Virginia

First Month 19, 1859

Dear Sarah,

Last night after we had all gone off to bed, there was a steady, insistent knocking on the door. Grandfather opened the door, with Father not far behind. They did not know but I was nearby. A tall man stood framed by the light of Grandfather's candle. The man asked, "Does a Friend live here?"

Grandfather replied, "Indeed he does. Come in." In stepped a man who by his appearance must have been a slave. He was muscular but looked as though he had not eaten for days. His clothes were torn and nearly falling off him. His shirt was in shreds and when he turned, Sarah, I saw scars and massive welts upon his back and shoulders. He must have been beaten many times.

Grandfather clasped the hand of the tall dark stranger and bid him come to the kitchen to eat. The man then turned to Grandfather and said, "I have my young'un with me. I had to make sure it was safe first."

Grandfather told him to bring the child inside. The man slipped out into the night, and moments later he returned with a frightened, half-frozen waif of a girl, who peeked out from behind him. "This here's Pearl," her father said. Grandfather stooped down to look directly into her eyes and said, "Pearl, you are safe here. Come and eat."

Mother cooked a grand breakfast—even though it was just after midnight. The little ones were sleeping but Father let me stay up. He asked me to help Mother cook. I have never seen people eat like they did. The man ate seven biscuits, six eggs, and more than a pound of our best bacon. At first Pearl just picked at her food. Finally her father told her, "Eat, child." Only then did she plow into the food on her plate. You would think these folks hadn't eaten in weeks.

After they ate, Mother brought out one of my favorite dresses and helped Pearl put it on. I was angry that Mother had not even asked me first. I scowled at Pearl and she knew I was upset. Then Mother asked Pearl if she wanted to rest, but Pearl was too frightened to leave her father's side.

The men moved to a corner of the room to talk. Mother tried to speak with Pearl, but she was just a mealy-mouthed child who would say nothing. I was more interested in what Grandfather had to say, anyway. He told Pearl's father, who goes by the name of Joseph, that there was presently too much snow for him to cross the river. Passage could not be arranged for another six weeks. Grandfather told Joseph that he and Pearl were welcome to hide out at Evergreen until they could safely continue their journey. I saw real gratitude in Joseph's eyes but Pearl was another story. She sat, sullen as could be while Mother tried to be nice to her. Imagine six weeks with her hiding out here at Evergreen!

Father motioned to Mother, who came near to him at the washing sink. I brought the plates over to the sink so I could hear what they were saying. I heard Father tell Mother that he was worried about being found out. People were watching Grandfather's every move. Hiding two slaves on the farm for six weeks in the dead of winter would be a challenge.

This made me even more angry. Great. Two slaves. One wearing my favorite dress. Both eating our food and staying on our farm for six long weeks while people are trying to catch Grandfather in the act of helping slaves escape. However are we to make it through this?

Grandfather then motioned for Joseph and Pearl to follow him up to the attic, where he had his drafting table, a small bed, and a chair. Quilts were piled in one corner. He showed them the little door under the eaves, where they were to hide if necessary. Grandfather would pull the bed over the door to hide it if trouble should come. He bade them a good night. Joseph, with downcast eyes, said, "Thank you, Master Taylor."

At that Grandfather turned around with great ferocity— so much in fact that Joseph and Pearl began to shake and I trembled with surprise. "I am not your master, Joseph. I am your friend. In this house you will call me Friend Yardley Taylor. Friend Yardley. And look up, man—look me in the eyes. You are special to God and therefore to me."

We were all shaking. I had never heard Grandfather's voice booming like that. Pearl wouldn't dare lift her head, and her shoulders were shaking with fear. Her father stood tall and shook Grandfather's extended hand. Joseph's hand was so large, it almost covered Grandfather's. "Thank you. Thank you, Mister Taylor, sir."

Grandfather then placed his other hand over Joseph's and said gently, "Yardley, sir. Friend Yardley."

Sarah, I could hardly sleep at all that night. How could I, knowing that two slaves were sleeping in the room above me? Yet, Sarah, I also could not get Grandfather's words out of my head. I must think more on this someday—once the slaves have left our home. Yes, then I will think about it.

The next morning, Grandfather told me the two had been running for months. They had left Oakwood Plantation on the Edisto River in South Carolina and spent months in forests and swamps, where they lived on berries and fish. Once it turned cold, they ran for weeks with only the North Star to guide them. Someone in Culpeper County told them that if they made it to Evergreen near the river, they could make it to freedom. In Winchester they overheard a man say he was going to the foundry at Evergreen in Goose Creek, and they knew that freedom was not far away.

The morning after that, Grandfather asked me to stay home from school. "Joshua will be suspicious," I told him. I did not want to be around Pearl and her father. I wanted things to be as they had always been. I wanted to go to school, meet Joshua at the corner, and walk with him as usual. Grandfather said, "I have already told your brother David to tell your teacher that you are needed at home today to help your Mother with the baby. She will be much too busy taking care of Joseph and Pearl. Hannah, we need to discuss this important turn of events. I spoke with Joseph last night and assured him he could trust us. His daughter is very frightened. Her mother died right before they began to run. You must do your part to help her feel welcome. Did you know that she is about your age?"

Sarah, can you imagine? Grandfather says Pearl is my age, but she is much too thin and feeble to be fifteen. Grandfather told me she has had a very difficult journey in life and we must provide her with Christian love and service. He was quite frank with me. Sarah, I do not think he approved of my frustration with Pearl being in our home, but I also do not think he understands that his actions could change all of our lives. Just a few months ago the trees in Goose Creek sported posters naming my grandfather, Yardley Taylor, as some awful criminal who helps slaves escape. Sarah, what are we to do?

Grandfather is going to Philadelphia to consult certain Friends there about this special case. He says he has never had a child come through before, and with the increased patrols and the suspicions about his involvement, he must be careful.

Tonight I will ask him to deliver this letter to you in person. It must not fall into the wrong hands. Please write back so Grandfather can bring me your counsel soon. I value your thoughts and wisdom, dear friend.

Anxiously I await your reply,

Hannah

Philadelphia, Pennsylvania

First Month 25, 1859

Dear Hannah,

I gave your Grandfather this special pot today when he left for Virginia. I have also enclosed a clipping Father found in the Philadelphia newspaper. You must be very careful, Hannah.

$250 REWARD

RUNAWAY FROM THE SUBSCRIBER FROM OAKWOOD PLANTATION ON THE EDISTO RIVER, DORCHESTER COUNTY, SOUTH CAROLINA, ON THE NIGHT OF 22ND SEPTEMBER LAST, HIS NEGRO MAN JOSEPH, A MAN OF FULL HEIGHT, VERY ERECT, ABOUT FORTY YEARS OF AGE. HE IS WELL SPOKEN AND CAN TELL A VERY PLAUSIBLE STORY. HE IS STOUTLY BUILT, STRONG WITH LARGE LIMBS, SIX FEET TWO INCHES HIGH, WEARING A BROWN WOOL JACKET AND DENIM BREECHES. ACCOMPANYING THE RUNAWAY IS HIS DAUGHTER, PEARL, ABOUT AGE 14, A BRIGHT AND SMART-LOOKING CHILD. IT IS SUPPOSED

THEY ARE MAKING THEIR WAY NORTH AND THAT THEY
WILL TRAVEL CHIEFLY AT NIGHT. THE ABOVE REWARD
WILL BE PAID UPON RETURN TO ME OR TO ANY JAIL IN
SOUTH CAROLINA.

BUCK WORTHY
CHARLESTON, S.C.

I know you are frightened and confused, but might it
not be that the Lord has placed you in this place at this time
for this very reason? I urge you to read the book of Esther in
the Bible, dear Hannah, for it may give you encouragement.

Your faithful friend,

Sarah

Goose Creek, Virginia

First Month 30, 1859

Dear Sarah,

I could not believe my eyes when I saw the advertisement in the newspaper you sent. Father says the advertisement also ran in the Leesburg newspaper. That is less than ten miles from here. What will we do?

I heard the patrols again last night. The dogs were yelping and barking as if they had cornered a possum. I knew it was not our charges, however. They were resting peacefully in our attic. I am not at peace, though, Sarah. I am greatly disturbed. I hope Grandfather returns soon with the plan proposed by the Friends on the committee there in Philadelphia. I hope the plan will be for them to move on very quickly now. After all, with the advertisements and the dogs, they should not stay with us a day longer. That is my opinion.

Mother does not agree. She notes that Pearl needs nourishment. Mother says she is weak from too many cold nights and not enough food. Pearl looks just fine to me. Mother does not believe she could survive a journey across the Catoctin Mountains in this cold weather. Father is concerned as well and talked with Mother about the secret room under the barn floor. Because of the cold, he does not want them to stay there unless absolutely necessary. But I can tell even Father is worried about the frequency of the dog patrols around Evergreen.

I am trying to be brave but it is difficult. Grandfather has drawn too much attention to us in the past few years by speaking out against slavery. The dangers are great. The penalties are severe. If Grandfather gets arrested this time, it is unlikely he will escape a sentence as before. The temper of the times is changing here in Virginia. Some say only bloodshed and war will solve this battle of words about liberty for slaves.

Joshua stopped by today. I was horrified. He just wanted to leave some mathematical equations for me to work on that would help our surveying work. I made an excuse for him to leave very quickly. I do not know where Joshua stands on this issue of aiding fugitive slaves. He is a fine young man, but he has never spoken about this with me. What if he were to find out and betray us? To an orphan a reward might be tempting.

I am deeply troubled in my spirit, Sarah. Please pray for me.

Your friend,

Hannah

Goose Creek, Virginia

Second Month 1, 1859

Dear Sarah,

Thank you for your letters that were hidden in our pot—
the one Grandfather brought back from Philadelphia—but
mostly what he brought back was news of the committee
and what they think we should do.

Late at night Grandfather and Father went to the attic to
discuss the plan with Joseph and Pearl. Grandfather showed
Joseph the advertisement. Neither Joseph nor Pearl could
read, but Joseph recognized that it was an ad for their
capture. Grandfather read the advertisement to them. At the
mention of Mister Buck Worthy's name, Joseph seemed to
grow cold. Grandfather noticed it and asked Joseph to tell
him more about the planter. Grandfather's sources in
Philadelphia had told him he was a successful planter near
the barrier islands of South Carolina and that Oakwood
Plantation was known for its superior long-staple cotton.

When Grandfather and Father came down again, they
told me and Mother what they had learned. "That Mister
Buck Worthy is one shrewd plantation owner!" exclaimed

Grandfather. Then he told me the story that Joseph had told him. "Master Worthy relied on his young daughter for news. She played in the kitchen under the watchful eye of the servants and then reported what she learned every night to her daddy. Master Worthy learned what his slaves were thinking from the house servants who talked in low tones while they shelled peas and cooked supper. That was how he found out that Joseph, his most valuable slave, was sweet on a slave girl on a plantation downriver. They had met at a Sunday worship gathering of slaves of neighboring plantations that was permitted by the plantation owners.

"Now, Master Worthy relied on Joseph to manage his 120 field slaves. He needed someone he could control, but someone who could keep the slaves from rebelling. Master Worthy saw how the other slaves respected Joseph. Also, Joseph had a way with the cotton crop. It seemed to increase under his care. Master Worthy had to find a way to keep Joseph bound to him so he would not consider running away. One day Master Worthy rode his horse to the cotton fields where Joseph was working and called him apart from the others. Frightened, Joseph asked 'Yes, Master?' Then Master Worthy told him he had bought Charity. The look in Joseph's eyes apparently told Mister Buck Worthy everything he needed to know. Joseph's loyalty could be bought through a family. And continued loyalty through keeping that family together."

I said, "I don't understand. Didn't the master do a good thing by buying Charity for Joseph?"

"Well," said Grandfather, "certainly Joseph and Charity were glad to be together, but they could not rest in the union. If Master Worthy could bring them together, then Master Worthy could tear them apart. He owned them both. He could sell one or the other at a moment's notice."

Grandfather continued with Joseph's story. "Though a slave marriage is not legally recognized in South Carolina, Master Worthy permitted Joseph and Charity to marry. Over the next several years Joseph was given increased privileges. He was respected by the slaves and worked as hard and as fast as any of them. If he came into a bit of meat from hunting, he would often share it with a slave who had been beaten or was sick. Master Worthy saw the wisdom of setting Joseph in charge of the rest of the slaves. The master often gave Joseph duties that took him into Georgetown, South Carolina. He had a special tag that permitted him to drive the wagon so if he was stopped, he could prove he had permission to be on the road. Under Joseph's watch the cotton continued to flourish.

"Joseph and Charity had children. Pearl is not the oldest. She has an older brother, William, and a younger sister, Talitha."

"Where are they?" I asked.

"I'm getting to that part of the story, but first let me tell you about Charity, Pearl's mother—a rare woman of the highest Christian devotion. Master Worthy wanted to buy Charity at any price. Charity's mother, Miriam, was a very strong Christian who named her three girls Charity, Grace, and Patience. She often told the girls that all three of those virtues would be required of them if they were to make it in the cruel world. Charity also had three brothers: Moses, Elijah, and Jeremiah. Charity's father had been sold farther south—some said New Orleans—when Charity was five years old. The plantation owner, Thomas Sutherland, ran into financial trouble and sold Charity's brothers and sisters to other plantation owners. Only Charity was left, as she was a favorite house servant of Mrs. Sutherland. When Master Worthy inquired as to the price for Charity, he was astonished at how high Mister Sutherland set the price, especially in light of his financial troubles. Nonetheless, Master Worthy bought Charity. She was his insurance policy for his cotton plantation."

Then Mother asked, "Did Joseph talk about his wife? Where is she now?"

Grandfather explained, "Charity loved Jesus and spent hours praying for her children and talking to them about him. She sang in the fields and she sang in the night. She sang songs of truth about the love of Jesus. Somehow, Joseph said, Charity knew she had to get those songs into the hearts of her children to give them strength. All went well until a few years ago, when William turned fifteen. He began to scorn his mother's Christian teaching as just a southern way to keep slaves in their place and began to talk about running away. Charity and Joseph begged him not to cause trouble for their family. William said that was just what Master Worthy wanted, and he wasn't going to give him the satisfaction. William tried to run away three times. Each time he was caught and severely whipped. Finally Master Worthy decided to sell William farther south. Joseph and Charity pleaded with the master, but he had determined that William was as much trouble as Joseph was good for his plantation. He turned a deaf ear to their pleas. Charity was pregnant with her fourth child at the time. That summer Charity became very ill with swamp fever that ravaged the plantation and she died. The baby she was carrying died with her."

"And her other child?" asked Mother.

"Ah," said Grandfather. "Talitha. She is only six now. When Joseph and Pearl ran away, they tried to bring Talitha. After William was sold and Charity and her unborn baby died, Master Worthy was afraid Joseph would have no reason to stay unless he kept his littlest daughter close at hand. Master Worthy took her into his home, in the care of his wife. Talitha's job was to stay up all night by the cradle of their little girl, Angelina. If the baby girl awoke, she was to rock her back to sleep so as not to disturb the slumber of the master and his wife. She was always under the Worthys' watchful eyes—in the master and mistress' bedchamber each night and as a house servant each day. When Joseph told me about this, I could tell that Pearl missed her sorely. I think she calls her 'Bookie' or some such thing."

Father added, "Anyway, the problem was that this plantation owner, Buck Worthy, believed that if he kept Talitha, then somehow he would have a hold on Joseph. After all, how could he leave the last child he had with his beloved wife? And besides, the plantation owner prided himself on never having a runaway slave who did not return—dead or alive. According to Joseph, he hires slave catchers to go after runaways, and he likely has one on their trail now."

Mother then said it was time for me to go to bed. For a long time I sat in the window looking out over the garden. I could not go to sleep. Not while Pearl and her father slept above my room. I could not stop imagining the sounds of dogs on their trail, men with guns, and little Talitha crying out for her family and no one there to comfort her. I remembered what Joshua had told me about orphans. I opened my Bible and found the place where God promises to care for orphans. "Lord, tonight watch over Talitha," I prayed. "Remember, God, you promised that when a father and mother are not there to care for their children, you will watch over them. Watch over little Talitha tonight, God. Keep her safe."

Sarah, I am still afraid and unsure. I guess I do want them to move on as soon as possible. Yet up until now this Railroad business did not have faces or names—names like Pearl or Joseph or little Talitha.

Forever your friend,

Hannah

Goose Creek, Virginia

Second Month 2, 1859

Dear Sarah,

I wrote you such a long letter last night, but today there is even more to report. Pearl is very ill. I rose this morning to take her and her father their breakfast. Mother had prepared a basket with bread, ham, milk, and dried peaches. Mother is quite concerned about Pearl's appetite. Pearl hardly weighs a thing and eats next to nothing. Mother told me this morning that she does not think Pearl is quite right.

Well, Mother was right. When I saw Pearl, even I knew there was something very wrong. I ran to get Mother, who tended to her right away. Pearl was blistering hot to the touch. Mother had me get cold water and cloths to bathe her forehead to get her fever down. I had a bowl of ice chips from the creek because Pearl could not seem to swallow even a sip of water. Her fever was so high that when I would slip an ice chip into her mouth, it seemed to melt straightaway. Joseph kept wringing his cap and pacing about. He told Mother this was how Charity looked right before she died.

I ran downstairs to alert Father and Grandfather. Grandfather saddled Frank and rode off to Doctor Janney's place. I told Father that Grandfather shouldn't take those kinds of chances, but Father assured me that Doctor Janney would not divulge our secret.

When Grandfather returned, he did not have Doctor Janney with him. He said that for the sake of precaution, he came first. Doctor Janney would come along shortly, as if paying his good friends a friendly, not a medical, visit. When Doctor Janney came, I led him up to the attic to where Pearl was lying on the bed. Mother was caring for her and trying to reduce her fever. Doctor Janney looked concerned as he examined Pearl. I came back down with him after his examination. He told Grandfather and Father that Pearl was very ill. She should not be moved and great care should be given to get some liquids into her. He remarked that Mother and I were giving her excellent care and should continue doing the same. He also left instructions for mustard plasters, snakeroot tea, and a medicinal concoction of a tablespoon of salt, the juice of a whole lemon, and castor oil. He said he would come again in a few days to check on her.

Your devoted friend,

Hannah

Philadelphia, Pennsylvania

Second Month 3, 1859

Dear Hannah,

A visitor came by last night and told Mother and Father that they should be expecting two packages from Virginia to arrive in a fortnight. I wish you could come, too. I understand your Grandfather will be transporting the packages to us. We will be waiting.

Your faithful friend,

Sarah

Goose Creek, Virginia

Second Month 5, 1859

Dear Sarah,

 Today Pearl was much worse. Mother and I took turns nursing her. I tried to get her to drink a little snakeroot tea, but she would only take the ice chips again. Mother sang to her, and I saw her curl up a little closer to Mother as she wiped her fevered brow. I could not help but think about how blessed I am to have a loving mother.

Appreciatively,

Hannah

Goose Creek, Virginia

Second Month 10, 1859

Dear Sarah,

Pearl is much better now. Her fever has broken. Doctor Janney came by today and said she is beyond danger, which gave Joseph much-needed relief. Doctor Janney discussed Grandfather's plan for the next part of their journey and said in *no* uncertain terms that Pearl could not go. She needs about two months' rest before she can make such a long and perilous journey to the North, and certainly she should not travel before spring.

Spring! Sarah, that is much too long a time. Someone is bound to find out who we are hiding here. Grandfather and Father have been speaking in hushed tones all morning. I can tell they are trying to figure out what to do next. Grandfather previously arranged with the committee in Philadelphia their safe passage north to Canada, if he can get our packages to the city. He had thought that would be no problem, until Pearl took ill.

Doctor Janney brought additional news. Apparently, he learned from Dr. Moore in Leesburg that a gentleman from

South Carolina has been asking at doctors' offices whether or not anyone has treated a tall Negro man with his daughter. The man from South Carolina is named Robert Blockett. Doctor Janney says it is likely he is nothing more than a slave catcher. Sarah, a slave catcher! Right here in our county, just miles from Evergreen. What if he comes to our home!

I must get these letters to you so you know what is happening. Uncle Oliver is going to Philadelphia in Grandfather's place while Grandfather figures out what to do next. I am giving him these letters right away, as he is leaving in just a few moments.

Your friend,

Hannah

Philadelphia, Pennsylvania

Second Month, 15, 1859

Dear Hannah,

I am so glad you were able to give your letters to your Uncle Oliver. I do believe this was the biggest pot yet, but then, dear Hannah, you had so much to tell me. I shared your letters with Mother and Father as well. Father has left with your Uncle Oliver to meet with those on the committee and devise a plan. He will carry the details of it back to your Grandfather. The committee is aware of this special case and will act soon, I am sure. Be patient, Hannah. Do not fear. Remember what our Lord has told us, "Let not your heart be troubled: ye believe in God, believe also in me."

Rest, Hannah, in this truth.

Your faithful friend,

Sarah

Goose Creek, Virginia

Second Month 19, 1859

Dear Sarah,

Uncle Oliver, Uncle Richard, Father, and Grandfather talked quietly most of the day. From what I understand, the committee thinks it best for Grandfather to get Joseph to Philadelphia as fast as possible. The committee is arranging passage for Joseph on to Canada, but it is taking some time with the passage for Pearl, as this is a special case. I imagine your mother and father are expecting the delivery of this package very soon. Sarah, I am quite frightened for Grandfather.

I will read the letter now that Uncle Oliver brought to me from you.

Ever your friend,

Hannah

Philadelphia, Pennsylvania

Second Month 16, 1859

Dear Hannah,

I can speak more frankly now because your Uncle Oliver is taking this letter back to you. Hannah, I know that my parents will be helping Joseph on to Canada. I am glad I will meet him. Because of your letters, I feel as though I know him. I hope Pearl will be all right without her father. She must be very frightened. Hannah, remember that she will have no one but you and your family once her father is gone. Try not to be afraid for yourself, but put yourself in Pearl's shoes.

Speaking of shoes, we are collecting as many pairs of good shoes as we can. So many of the packages that are delivered to us are in need of clothing and shoes. Our sewing circle is working our fingers to the bone sewing clothes for every man, woman, and child the Lord may send our way.

Hannah, you are involved now, whether you like it or not. I wonder if our Lord has not provided you a chance to see how he works in this Liberty Line. Think about what he said, dear Hannah: "I was hungry, and ye gave me meat: I was thirsty, and ye gave me drink: I was a stranger, and ye took me in: Naked, and ye clothed me: I was sick, and ye visited me. . . . Verily I say unto you, Inasmuch as ye have done it unto one of the least of these my bretheren, ye have done it unto me."

Maybe you will meet the Lord in Pearl and Joseph, dear Hannah.

Your faithful friend,

Sarah

Goose Creek, Virginia

Second Month 20, 1859

Dear Sarah,

I woke this morning and Grandfather was gone. So was Joseph. Father says Grandfather is taking Joseph across the Catoctin Mountains—a difficult journey for any man and much too difficult for a child who has been ill. Pearl is here. Grandfather left me a note:

Dearest Hannah,
I know you are troubled. Do not fear. Be strong. Your help is now needed. You must care for our special guest as I would. Obey your parents. Love your enemy.

Your Grandfather

Mother and Father told me that Uncle Oliver will tell others that Grandfather has taken off on another of his nursery expeditions. Uncle Oliver learned of a new variety of ginkgo tree that is arriving in Philadelphia soon by ship. Everyone knows how excited Grandfather gets when a new species of tree or plant comes to America. Uncle Richard will take over the United States mail route until Grandfather returns. It may be weeks. After I read Grandfather's note, Mother asked me to take Pearl her breakfast and give her a message from her father, who slipped away while Pearl was sleeping.

Pearl jumped a foot high off the bed when I opened the door. Her eyes darted around the room and she looked at me in fear. I put down the basket of bread and fruit, folded my arms across my chest, and said, "Your father left in the middle of the night with my Grandfather. Your father said to tell you that he will see you in Freedom Land—at the end of the Liberty Line."

Sarah, we both just stood there staring at each other. Neither of us knew what to do. Finally I turned and left the room. That Pearl is one strange girl. When I came back downstairs, Mother and Father explained that Pearl will be my special charge until she is strong enough to make the trip herself. They told me I am to do all I can to prepare her for a life of freedom and for the challenges ahead. What in the world could they mean? This child won't even talk.

I am tired and I miss Grandfather. Oh, how I wish things were back the way they were. I don't want to be brave or strong.

Your sad friend,

Hannah

Goose Creek, Virginia

Second Month 24, 1859

Dear Sarah,

You will think me frightful. I could not stand it a moment longer. This scared young slip of a girl won't talk. Day in and day out I take her food. I talk to her. I ask her if she needs anything. She says nothing. I ask about her health. She does not respond. She is a sullen, unthankful girl—after all my family is doing to help her and her father.

Today when I took her breakfast, she once again refused to say one word. That is when I decided that even if Grandfather is angry with me, I do not care. I have to get her to talk.

"So, who is Bookie?"

Her eyes got wide and she cocked her head to one side.

"Come on, Pearl, don't you know Bookie? Grandfather told me about your sister. I know all about her. She's six years old and you had to leave her behind when you ran away."

Pearl turned from me but I saw tears in her eyes. Well, Sarah, at least I was getting a reaction from her. I continued, "She's with that mean Master Worthy, isn't she? No way for her to escape, right, Pearl?"

I saw Pearl's shoulders shake. She must have been crying but she still kept it inside. She still wouldn't utter a sound.

"She won't see the end of the Liberty Line, will she? Why . . . she will never see the Underground Railroad train come for her. She's all alone. No mother. No father. No brother. And no sister. Poor Bookie."

Pearl twirled around, looked me in the eye, and, opening and closing her fists, which she held tight to her side, she said, "Her name . . . is Tookie."

I was so excited, I almost danced a little jig right there. Pearl had finally spoken!

"Tookie—now, that's a great name. I thought your father told my parents her name was Talitha."

"Talitha her given name. Tookie my name for her. Talitha from the Bible."

"What does Talitha mean?" I asked.

Peal shrugged. "Don't rightly know. Mammy picked it." Then Pearl sat on the bed and sobbed. "Got to find a way to get Tookie out of there. Master Worthy ain't never going to let her go. He watches over her day and night. He works her so hard. She has to watch Master's girl-child all night long. Why, Tookie is just a girl-child herself! She should be sleeping in the night, not staying awake. Master ties her to the cradle and to a bell. If Tookie lays down and tries to sleep at night, the bell rings. Then Master whips her. If the baby cries, Tookie has to rock her back and forth till she falls asleep again."

I asked, "Do you think Master Worthy would sell Tookie?"

Pearl said, "No, don't think he aim to do that. He want power over Pappy. He want Pappy to try to come back and get Tookie. Then he gonna get Pappy."

"Do you think your father would do that? Get to freedom and then turn around and go back to the slave country for Tookie?"

"I know he gonna do that. That's what he told me every day in the swamp. First he was gonna get me to freedom, then he was gonna come back to get Tookie."

"Pearl, that's too dangerous. He'll get caught."

"I know, Miss Hannah. But I don't think Pappy can live with hisself, knowing Tookie still with Master Worthy and he be in freedom."

Then she lowered her head and said very quietly, "Miss Hannah, do you think Pappy will come back for me?"

I realized that in the hurry of all the plans about Joseph, no one had told Pearl about the plans for her to join him. I explained about the committee and told her all about you, Sarah. I said that one day soon, when she was strong enough, Grandfather would make sure she got to your home in Philadelphia. I told her about you and your parents and what you do with packages when they arrive. I told her about Canada. I am so glad you told me so much about the settlements in Canada. I told her there are many, many American slaves living free lives in Canada and that she should not be afraid.

Then, Sarah, do you know what she said? Pearl said, "If I could just be brave like you, Miss Hannah."

Brave like me? Sarah, I am jelly on the inside. You would have been proud of me. I told Pearl that she must be brave and strong because it is the only way she can help Tookie. Pearl seemed satisfied and began to eat her breakfast. Sarah, we have to make a plan. We have to help Tookie come north to join her father and her sister. Please ask your parents what we can do.

Your humbled friend,

Hannah

Philadelphia, Pennsylvania

Third Month 4, 1859

Dear Hannah,

There is much excitement here as we wait for your Grandfather and his companion. We expect them any day now. Father has met several times with the committee to plan the next part of his journey and to plan for Pearl's journey as well. The plans for helping a girl traveling alone are quite tricky, and they are taking extra special care to think this through. Hannah, I think I am going to like Pearl.

I shared your letter with Mother and Father. We all prayed together about Tookie. Father said this would be a challenge, but one he is anxious to take on. He will raise this situation with the committee when he next meets with them. Hannah, do you remember how I told you there are some on the committee who travel in the South posing as slave owners to purchase slaves who are relatives of those they have already helped to freedom? Perhaps this is how we can rescue Tookie. Mother said it may require a fund. She has some ideas for how we can raise the money. I do wish you would come soon so we can work on this together. However, I understand that you are needed there.

You must help Pearl get ready. Father told me that the committee will have to be extra careful in arranging passage for her. A slave catcher hired by Master Worthy may be thrown off the trail because he is looking for a father and daughter traveling together. Yet soon he will realize they have separated. A girl traveling alone is much more suspicious. It will take great planning to make sure Pearl joins her father in Canada.

Now, did you notice that this is the ninth square I have sent to you? Perhaps we will finish this quilt after all.

Your always-stitching friend,

Sarah

Goose Creek, Virginia

Third Month 5, 1859

Dear Sarah,

Things are going much better with Pearl now that she is talking. I am learning much about her time in South Carolina. Sarah, you cannot imagine what she has seen. Her stories sometimes make me laugh. One day Pearl told me she thinks the way I call the hogs is funny. In South Carolina they say, "Souie, souie" or "Sook, sook." Pearl told me that one of her duties at Oakwood Plantation was to slop the hogs. A few weeks before they left, Pearl thought a boy named Joel might be getting sweet on her. Every day he would follow her to the pigpen just to try to talk to her. Finally Pearl asked Joel, "Mister, you follow me morning and night to this pigpen. Do you happen to be in love with one of these pigs? If so, I'd like to know which one it is, so I can tell that pig about your affections." Pearl and I laughed until we thought our sides would split.

She told me she lived in a little cabin with a mattress on the floor. The mattress was made out of ticking fabric filled with cornhusks. I tried to imagine what that must feel like,

Sarah. Her mammy and pappy, as she calls them, got a ration of food each week from the master of the plantation. It wasn't enough to feed a family, but they made do by catching rabbits and possums and tending a garden. Pearl told me they worked the garden at night because they tended the cotton fields by day.

Sarah, that isn't all. It turns out that if one of the slaves died, they had to have the funeral at night. They were not allowed to stop work for any reason unless it was the Sabbath or Christmas Day.

On the Sabbath, the mistress of the plantation made sure all the slave children had a sort of Sunday school. They were taught Scriptures—not to read, mind you, as that was against the law. But they were taught passages of the Bible, which Pearl said she tried to commit to memory as best she could. Sarah, Pearl is really bright. She just needs someone to help her. She quoted the entire text of Psalm 23 to me just as it is in the Bible. Think what she could do if she learned to read and write.

Later in the day on the Sabbath, the slaves would gather near the creek for their own worship service. You cannot imagine what the slave worship services are like. They are as loud and lively as ours are quiet and silent. They dance and lift their hands to heaven. They clap and sway while they sing. We don't even sing! I find my heart strangely warmed to this idea of body, mind, and spirit all worshiping together at the same time.

I asked Pearl how old she is. She doesn't rightly know. She imagines she is about fourteen, but she doesn't know for sure. I asked her what month and day she was born. She doesn't know that either. She did tell me that if sold, she would be worth about $1,000. Seems to me that is not the right number for her to know. She should know her age, in my humble opinion. Would that be how much we'd have to raise to buy Tookie, I wonder?

Your definitely fifteen-year-old friend,

Hannah

Hannah

Philadelphia, Pennsylvania

Third Month 8, 1859

Dear Hannah,

Your grandfather has arrived! Joseph is with him. They traveled up the mountain range through western Pennsylvania rather than the regular way. Your grandfather said he had to be especially careful with the slave catcher on his heels. Have you heard any more about Robert Blockett, the slave catcher? Your grandfather told us he is known to be quite determined, and he takes pride in his ability to return property alive to the masters of the southern plantations. It is so good to be with your grandfather. No wonder you are so happy when you are together. He is full of strength and courage.

Joseph stayed with us for only one night. It was too dangerous for him to stay longer, because of the connection between our two families. I am glad I got to speak with him. I told him what I had learned about Pearl from you. He seemed glad to hear that she is feeling better and getting stronger. He is anxious to have her begin her journey to freedom, as well. He wants you to tell Pearl that he loves her and he will never be happy until she is with him again in Freedom Land. That is what he calls Canada. Your grandfather should return soon. He and Father are meeting with the committee tomorrow to make plans. I told Friend Yardley what you learned from Pearl about Tookie. He seemed thoughtful and didn't say much then. Later I heard him tell Mother that he is proud of you for taking an interest in Pearl and her sister. They are going to talk with the committee about Tookie tomorrow, as well. Your grandfather said I might see you soon. I wonder what he has in mind.

I'll write again as soon as I have some more news. Tomorrow Mother and I are meeting with our sewing circle to make more clothes. I am happy to say I gave Joseph two new shirts I sewed all by myself. Mother gave him shoes that can stand the cold of the North, and a coat and two pairs of pants. The committee will let us know when he reaches Canada. He has begun his journey. All I know is they are sending him from farm to farm. All else is secret.

Your friend,

Sarah

Philadelphia, Pennsylvania

Third Month 10, 1859

Dear Hannah,

Your grandfather is on his way home to you with the letter I wrote yesterday. This letter will go by regular post inside my tenth square. Yes, I am finding time, with all I have to sew for the Railroad, to work on our quilt. I think we will finish it by fall.

Mother and Father told me last night that the committee agrees an attempt will be made to purchase Talitha from Master Worthy. They believed he may see Talitha as a way to entice Joseph back to his plantation, and he may refuse any offer for her purchase. We must pray, dear friend, for Talitha to join her family.

I think your grandfather may bring you to Philadelphia for a visit soon. He did find time to purchase several new varieties of plantings. He said you will be most happy to see the treasures he has bought. He is just like you when it comes to talking about spring. He loves the planting season. I think he is planning another purchasing trip soon. Oh, how I would love to see you, my dearest friend.

Forever your faithful quilter,

Sarah

Goose Creek, Virginia

Third Month 12, 1859

Dear Sarah,

Mother has asked me to try to help Pearl learn to read and at least write her name. Mother says that as long as Pearl is with us, we must do all we can to prepare her for her new life. She says I can teach Pearl how to write her name and that we should give her a good Quaker name, as a necessary diversion should anyone question her.

I took a slate and chalk up to the attic to begin our first lesson. I have never seen such a scared little girl. I told Pearl I will teach her letters first and wrote on the slate in large print the letters *A, B, C.* You would have thought I had printed the name of the Devil himself. Pearl began to shake and whimper. Sarah, I thought, *I will never be able to teach this child anything. She just has no gumption.* I said, "Fine. If you want to get caught by the slave catchers, that's your choice."

When I came downstairs, I told Mother what happened. Mother asked me to sit down and told me a story that Joseph had told her. "Pearl was a little girl about six years old. One day the master's children were playing nearby. She often played with them. That day the master's son, Toby, was stacking three wooden blocks, each with a letter on it—*A, B, C.* Pearl sat down with Toby and played with the blocks, stacking them and knocking them down. Master Worthy came by on his horse, jumped down, and knocked the blocks out of Pearl's hands. He then took his whip and whipped her seven good lashes, till the blood was streaming down her back. Charity and Joseph were both out in the cotton fields. Pearl went to an old mammy there, who nursed her wounds. Pearl didn't understand what had happened and never went near Toby again. But it wasn't Toby, Hannah—it was the letters on the blocks."

Mother explained that it is against the law to teach slaves to read or write. I felt terrible, Sarah, for judging Pearl so. There is so much I don't understand. I went back upstairs with the slate wiped clean of any letters. I took a Bible instead. I sat on the bed next to Pearl.

"Your father says that your mother used to sing to you about Jesus. Would you like me to read to you about Jesus?" I asked. Pearl nodded. "The disciples thought Jesus needed to work on very important matters, and they became annoyed that mothers were bringing their children to see Jesus. Do you know what he said to his friends?" Pearl shook her head and pulled the covers up tight under her chin. "Well listen to this! Jesus said, 'Suffer the little children to come unto me, and forbid them not: for of such is the kingdom of God.' Isn't that great, Pearl? Jesus wants us to come to him. Do you know how to spell *Jesus*? It's right here. Do you want to look?"

Pearl scooted closer to me and looked at the place in the book where I had my finger right at the name *Jesus*. "Would you want to learn to spell *Jesus*?" Pearl nodded. I then took my slate and wrote the letter *J*. Pearl traced it with her finger. She still didn't speak. Then I wrote the letter *E*. Pearl traced that letter with her finger. I wrote the letters *S* and *U* and *S*, and she traced all the letters with her finger. I then gave her the chalk and she looked up inquisitively at me. "Go ahead. You try," I told her. Pearl then very carefully and painstakingly tried her best to write the name *Jesus*. It looked like this:

JESUS

It was a bit scratchy but I praised Pearl anyway. "Did you know that Jesus talked about a pearl once?" I said. Pearl seemed to brighten but she still wouldn't say anything. I turned to the book of Matthew and read, 'The kingdom of heaven is like unto a merchant man, seeking goodly pearls: who, when he had found one pearl of great price, went and sold all that he had, and bought it.'

"There is the same letter in the name *Pearl* as in *Jesus*. Do you see it?" I asked Pearl. Pearl smiled as she pointed to the letter *E*. She took the slate and wrote the letter *E* again and gave it back to me. I filled in the rest of the letters of her name. She took the slate and stared at her name a long time, and then, Sarah, she smiled at me!

Suddenly Mother appeared at the door. "Quick. Into the little room." She opened the door in the eaves and Pearl ducked inside. Mother quickly made up the bed and pushed it in front of the door. I heard what Mother had heard—the dog patrol. Oh, how I wished Grandfather and Father were home. With one last look, Mother left the room. Carrying my slate and Bible, I followed her downstairs. No sooner had Mother settled back in her chair and picked up her needlework and I had placed my slate and Bible down on the table than we heard a loud, long knocking at the door.

I was terrified. I looked at Mother with fear but she signaled me to be brave. Sarah, Mother is so strong and so courageous but I was shaking inside. Mother opened the door. A tall dark-haired man with a scar on his cheek stood with his hat in his hands. "Morning, Ma'am. My name is Robert Blockett. I work for a Mister Buck Worthy, owner of Oakwood Plantation in South Carolina. Mister Worthy is missing some property that we believe might be hiding out in this area."

Mother acted confused. "Property?"

"Yes, two slaves. A father named Joseph ran off several months ago with his daughter Pearl. We tracked them to Culpeper, Virginia, Ma'am. The sheriff there told us about your place here. Seems like a number of the runaways have stopped by Evergreen before."

"Well, as you can see, sir, this is a home for myself and my children, who are otherwise engaged, so I bid you goodbye."

Mister Blockett looked inside. I thought he could see right through me. As his eyes scanned the room, I noticed that my slate was facing up with the name *Pearl* written on it. I thought, *Oh no, what if he sees it?* My heart was racing as he looked around the room. I moved so I would block his view of the table, where my slate was. After surveying the room, Mister Blockett continued, "That's not what I hear. Doesn't Yardley Taylor live here?"

"Yes. He is my father."

"Well, what I hear is that Mister Taylor has caused quite some consternation in a number of the neighboring counties over the years. The sheriff in Fauquier County told me he has led raids to free slaves in their county. In fact, Sheriff Thompson told me he would be happy to lend me some slave-hunting hounds. But I told him mine are better and have tracked these two for many miles and won't be giving up too soon."

"Sir, what you speak of—these accusations—were made many years ago."

"Are you saying they have no merit?"

"I am saying that these accusations have nothing to do with the so-called property you seek. I imagine they are long gone to freedom by now."

"Oh, perhaps, but then again, they could be just within spitting distance from here," he said as he stared coldly at me. "Good day for now, Ma'am." He tipped his hat to Mother, put it back on his head, and mounted his horse. As he rode off, he turned his horse back, stopped, and stared up at the attic. Could he know?

I ran to Mother and buried my head in her shoulder. I was so frightened. "Mother, I don't like that man one bit. He's going to be back. I know he is. Whatever will we do?"

Mother's eyes were flashing but she stood for several minutes at the door, listening to the sound of Mister Blockett's horse galloping away. Then she spoke calmly. "Hannah, we must move quickly. Follow me." Mother and I walked down to the barn, where Mother swept away the hay over the trapdoor. Mother told me that we must help Pearl to this place tonight at nightfall, after David and the baby were asleep. I stared into the gaping hole. A small ladder leaned against the side. Mother beckoned me to go down and she followed. We freshened the muslin cloth and stuffed it with new hay for Pearl's bed. Mother took a quick inventory of supplies that would be needed.

"Mother, won't it be too cold for Pearl here?"

"No, you would be surprised how a home in the earth even at this time of year can be warm. There are extra blankets for the horses. We will put some down here as well. There are dried peaches, apples, some salted ham, and a jug of water. We will bring Pearl other food each day."

When we climbed back out of the tiny room under the floor of the barn, Mother pulled the door back down on the floor and swept hay over it. "Now, Hannah, you must be very careful to do exactly as I do." Mother then picked up cow dung and spread it around the door.

"Mother!" I exclaimed. "What in the world are you doing?"

"It throws the dogs off the scent of a human, Hannah. This is very important. Hay alone covering the trapdoor is not enough. And bring in one of the cows. Fresh dung is better. Now, Hannah, you must not forget."

Sarah, I am frightened.

Your friend,

Hannah

Goose Creek, Virginia

Third Month 13, 1859

Dear Sarah,

Last night Mother and I waited until after dark, when the other children were asleep, to move Pearl. We were barely down from the attic room when we heard the sounds of the dog patrols coming down the road. Sounded like three, maybe four, hounds. Then I heard horses. I pushed Pearl down the gravel path to the barn as fast as I could. I swept away the hay, pushed a cow out of the way, and helped Pearl down the ladder into the dark chamber. I urged her to stay still and be very quiet, no matter what happened. I closed the trapdoor and brushed the hay all over it. I pulled another cow from the water trough outside the barn. The more animals, the better, I thought. It would confuse the dogs. Then I remembered what Mother had told me. I prodded the cow dung with a stick until some of it covered where the door was. Good old Bessie cooperated and delivered a pile of fresh dung right where I needed it. I rushed back to the house and came in the back way.

No sooner was I inside than the sheriff arrived with Mister Blockett. That man gives me the willies, Sarah. His eyes are as black as coal, and that scar on his cheek—well, I don't want to think about how he got that. Father asked, "What is the meaning of this?"

The sheriff responded, "I know you are a good man, Thomas Brown, but the activities of your father-in-law, Mister Yardley Taylor, are in serious question. There is a rumor that two slaves made their way from Fauquier County to your home here at Evergreen—a father and a daughter. Mister Blockett here has been hired by Mister Worthy of South Carolina to bring back his property. I'm afraid we must search your home, Thomas."

"Do you have the proper warrants?" asked Father. The sheriff showed him the documents. "Go ahead," said Father, standing aside from the door. "You will find nothing out of order here."

Sarah, my heart was pounding so hard that I just knew they could hear it. After they didn't find anyone in the house, Mister Blockett stared at me. I know my face was rosy from the crisp, cool air, but I was hoping he wouldn't notice. "Check the barn and the creek," he said. Oh, Sarah, I have never prayed so hard. I prayed for Pearl, that she would not be afraid. I prayed for the Lord to confuse those dogs. And I prayed for my hands to stop shaking. Mother and Father and I stood out on the porch to watch them. The dogs yelped all the way to the barn as if they were on the trail of a runaway slave, just as they had been trained. Of course, they were on a trail. We had just been there. I leaned in closer to Mother, who held me tightly to her side. We saw them approach the barn— the sheriff with his rifle, and Mister Blockett with his dogs. The dogs were yelping and straining at their leashes. As soon as they got inside the barn, however, the dogs ran in circles, confused, disoriented. It seemed as if the trail had gone cold at the door of the barn. The sheriff and Mr. Blockett checked the creek in the next field. Soon they were back on our front porch. Mister Blockett narrowed his eyes and said, "Where is Mister Taylor tonight?"

Father replied, "Mister Taylor is in Philadelphia, where he goes every year at this time to purchase seedling trees and plants for the nursery." I was still trembling but Mother held me tighter, as if to say, "Courage, Hannah. Take courage."

Mister Blockett and the sheriff mounted their horses and rode off. When we came inside, Mother had me sit by the fire. She warmed a cup of sassafras tea to calm me down, but I was shaking too hard. I wanted desperately to check on Pearl but Mother and Father would not allow it. Mother held me in her lap. Even though I am big now, I did not mind one whit. I wanted the comforting of a mother more than ever before. Mother and Father told me they were very proud of me.

Father said it was time I learned more about the Underground Railroad and Grandfather's involvement over the last twenty years with antislavery activities. Father explained that for many years Grandfather had been outspoken about the right of slaves to be free. He had worked tirelessly in a public way as president of antislavery organizations. Mother explained that Grandfather had also worked very hard in a less public way, by actively helping many slaves find their way to Pennsylvania and on to freedom. As I already knew, sometimes that meant slaves stayed here at Evergreen. Much of this work had been accomplished late at night, without us children knowing. There was a need for absolute secrecy. Father told me that Friend Samuel Janney, principal of your Springdale School next door, has faced much opposition as he has tried to lay out arguments against slavery, in newspapers. The Quaker Friends in this area will not stand for the owning of one person by another. But this view is not popular in Loudoun County of the Commonwealth of Virginia.

Father explained that Grandfather was most hopeful that I would assist him in his activities, as he is getting older. Old experience and youthful energy, Grandfather always said, were the best combination. Grandfather had been disappointed when I resisted the idea. I told Father it made me sad to disappoint Grandfather, but I thought it was wrong to bring so much trouble to our family to help people we don't even know.

Mother said, "You are getting to know Pearl, now aren't you?"

"Yes," I replied, "but I will be very happy when she moves on from here. I think I will like her much better once she is in Canada."

Mother smiled at Father and said, "Well, Hannah, dear, we will not ask you to do more than you are willing, but we did want you to understand that helping fugitive slaves runs long and deep in our family. Your Grandfather loves you so much that he wanted you to share his work with him. But you must decide for yourself what you are willing to sacrifice to do that. We cannot make you choose to give up your security for that of another. We are proud that you would help us today. You may have saved Pearl's life tonight."

Mother told me that the most important thing we can do for Pearl now is to prepare her for her journey. Mother said that strengthening her with food is good, but now we must teach her to avoid capture. When I asked how, Mother explained that the best disguise is one no one expects. I was confused, but Mother explained that everyone will be looking for a poor, uneducated young girl, unsure of herself and frightened. "We must work with Pearl to give her courage," said Mother. "The best way to give her courage is to give her the ability to persuade others of her new identity." I was still confused, so Mother opened a trunk and pulled out a composition book and a book of letters. "I used these when I taught at Oakdale years ago. I want you to have them now. Help Pearl learn to read and write and quickly, Hannah. Oh, and we must give her a new name. Let's call her Polly. Now, she needs a new last name. What will it be?"

I knew immediately. "Williams," I said, "after her brother."

Sarah, I don't know how much time we have. Grandfather should be here soon with the plan of the committee. I need to help Pearl learn how to pretend to be a free Black in just a short amount of time. Oh, Lord, please help me.

Your exhausted friend,

Hannah

Goose Creek, Virginia

Third Month 16, 1859

Dear Sarah,

Grandfather is back. I did miss him. He is full of news. He says, that by now Joseph should be in New York State and crossing over into Canada. Grandfather says the committee is working on the plan for Pearl but it may not be ready for another month. Another month, Sarah! That is much too long. What if Mister Blockett comes back? Surely, the committee does not expect us to keep Pearl here that long?

I have been helping Pearl with her writing, each day after I come from school. She can write her name *Pearl* now with ease. She is struggling a bit with the new name *Polly* but understands it is for her safety. She was surprised that I chose her last name, but she agreed it was perfect. I told her that at least her new name has lots of l's in it, so if we are short on time for her to learn to read and write, she can make lots of pretty loops in writing *Polly Williams*. Mother told me I must teach her cursive, as this would be the way a free, educated black girl in the North would write.

Pearl asked about Tookie. Have you heard anything else?

Devotedly,

Hannah

Philadelphia, Pennsylvania

Third Month 18, 1859

Dear Hannah,

I am afraid I have bad news. The committee wrote to Master Worthy to seek the purchase of Talitha. Master Worthy responded with a resounding no. He said he would not sell her at any price. The committee wrote again and offered eight hundred dollars, but he turned them down flat. Do not say anything to Pearl yet, as Father is working with the committee on another plan. Meanwhile Mother says we should begin the fund anyway. She and I have planned a bazaar for Fourth Month, Eighth Day. Mother is soliciting many articles by telling the story of Pearl and Talitha. Their story has captured the hearts of our sewing circle. We are still making clothes for the fugitives. The need is great. But we are also sewing silk purses and scarves for sale at the bazaar.

Hannah, ask your grandfather if he is coming to Philadelphia next month. Perhaps he could bring you to visit in time for the bazaar.

Your friend,
Sarah

Goose Creek, Virginia

Third Month 20, 1859

Dear Sarah,

The lessons continue in earnest. Every day when I get home from school, Pearl and I work on her writing and reading. She is able to write her new name very well now. Mother has worked with her hair to make it appear more stylish. Mother and I laugh at this because we Quakers are not known for style.

The most difficult thing for me to help Pearl with is the way she speaks. Frankly, Sarah, she sounds very southern. In fact, she sounds downright South Carolinian. She told me today that she could help me tote the buckets up from the springhouse. I told her she could do no such thing. She could help me *carry* the buckets but no toting was allowed. She calls her old master "marster", and she calls women "missus". She calls her father "Pappy" and her mother "Mammy". Actually, I think it is funny when she asks about my Grandpappy. I have started to call Grandfather that when I am teasing him. He says he doesn't know who is teaching whom what!

I am amazed we have been able to keep Pearl's presence here a secret. Joshua is around more and more, but Uncle Richard keeps him busy at the foundry during the afternoon when I am teaching Pearl. Doctor Janney visited Pearl last week. He says she may be ready for the journey in a month. Sarah, I have so much to do. Only one month to teach Pearl to read.

Grandfather is considering your request to bring me to the bazaar. Mother has been working on some needlework for the bazaar just in case.

Your friend forever,

Hannah

Philadelphia, Pennsylvania

Third Month 21, 1859

Dear Hannah,

The committee told Father that their sources in South Carolina said Master Worthy was angry when he got news from his slave catcher, Blockett, about Joseph going to Canada. Then he doubled the bounty for Pearl. There is a bonus for Mister Blockett if he can catch Pearl before she gets out of the slaveholding states, so please be careful, Hannah. He still refuses to sell Tookie but says that if he were to sell her, he might do so for $1,300. Mother says, then that is what we must earn from the bazaar. It is a terribly large amount of money.

Be of good cheer, Hannah we are on the Lord's side.

Your friend with many pricked
fingers from too much sewing,

Sarah

Goose Creek, Virginia

Third Month 23, 1859

Dear Sarah,

I can come! Grandfather must see your Uncle Robert for more reprints of his Loudoun County map, and he is also eager to revisit the nurseries there that have such unusual plantings and cuttings. I think Mother has been working on him, too. I threw my arms around him and said, "Oh, thank you, dear Grandpappy." Grandfather threw back his head and laughed. I think his new name will stick, Sarah.

Mother will take over Pearl's lessons while I am gone. All seems quiet here. Word has it that Mister Blockett is still up north somewhere, hoping to get word on Pearl from the other slave catchers and bounty hunters. He assumes she is on the same Liberty Line as her father, just a bit farther behind. Mother told me I must write to her every day.

We leave tomorrow for our journey. I will be with you again soon, dear Sarah. I miss you so much. This will be wonderful!

Your friend,

Hannah

Philadelphia, Pennsylvania

Fourth Month 1, 1859

Dear Father and Mother,

It is so wonderful to be with Sarah and her family. They send their love and hope that we can all be together again soon. We are busy getting ready for the bazaar. Many items have been donated or made just for this fair to secure Tookie's release. Mother, it is so different here. There are Negro men and women who move about freely and have jobs. They are able to live with their families, without fear of someone being sold. I am beginning to see now what Sarah is speaking about. Tonight at dinner Sarah's father explained that the delivery business for them has become more difficult, as the numbers of packages have increased since the passage of the Fugitive Slave Act. Now, even though the Smiths live in a free state, they could be fined or jailed or both if caught assisting a runaway slave.

Grandfather has been meeting with the committee about our special charge and the plans for reuniting Pearl with her father. Joseph is now safely in Canada at the St. Catharine Settlement. Tomorrow Grandfather is taking me with him to the nursery here, to help select plants. Mother, I do so love being with Grandfather.

Mother, you will be pleased to see that this letter is carefully hidden in our latest quilting square. Sarah and I made this one together just to show you that I am not neglecting my needlework. I know you think I am frightfully inept at such things. It's just that I would rather be outside with Grandfather in the garden with the sun and dirt and plants than inside with thread and fabric and needles.

I will write again soon with all the news. We are working tirelessly on the bazaar and hope to earn the money to secure Tookie's release. Wouldn't that be a wonderful surprise for Pearl? Sarah's father said that Master Worthy is still unwilling to deal with the pretend slave owner. Her father suspects that Master Worthy knows an abolitionist is behind this inquiry of sale. Nonetheless, Sarah and I continue to believe that nothing will keep this family apart, and we will do everything we can to make sure the money is there if Master Worthy relents and releases Tookie for sale.

I miss you, dearest Mother and Father. I love you so very much.

Your faithful daughter,

Hannah

Philadelphia, Pennsylvania

Fourth Month 4, 1859

Dear Father and Mother,

It is very late but I must write you. I am sure you will hear of it soon in the newspapers. Today a man, a Negro from Loudoun County—our county in Virginia—was arrested and brought here to Philadelphia! His name is Daniel Webster, but they say his real name when he lived in Virginia was Daniel Dangerfield. He was arrested under the Fugitive Slave Act and is to be returned to his owner in Virginia. There is great outrage here. The Smith home was filled with people discussing what they should do to assist this poor man.

Mister Dangerfield has lived in Harrisburg, Pennsylvania, (where he was arrested) for nine years. He has a wife and two children. But Mother, it is so sad—both of the children have died. He buried one child just last week. They say he belonged to a Mister French Simpson of Loudoun and had worked for him near Aldie. Sarah's father said that Mister Simpson's widow, Mrs. Elizabeth Simpson, authorized the warrant. Mother, have you heard of Mrs. Simpson?

Apparently, Mister J. H. Gulick, who is also from Loudoun and works for the Simpsons, came with the marshal to the early-morning market near where Mister Dangerfield lives, and grabbed him. The marshal yelled out to the crowd that Dangerfield was a thief. He did this, Grandfather surmises, to keep the crowd from trying to rescue Daniel Dangerfield right then and there. The marshal handcuffed the poor man and took him to Philadelphia for a hearing, the outcome of which could be this poor man's return back to slavery.

A steady stream of people arrived here at the Smiths' tonight, talking about what they can do to help. Oh, we must pray for this dear man and his wife. What sorrows they have faced, with the recent deaths of their two children. What more sorrow they would face if Mister Dangerfield is sent back to slavery.

Your daughter,

Hannah

Philadelphia, Pennsylvania

Fourth Month 5, 1859

Dear Father and Mother,

We went to First Day services but there was not much silence today. Many spoke out vigorously about Mister Dangerfield's predicament. There was much prayer for justice and righteousness to prevail. Grandfather also spoke out. He had fire in his eyes. Moved by the Spirit as I have never seen him, he spoke of God's view of man as just a little lower than the angels and said all men, no matter what their color, are loved by God. Grandfather spoke boldly and said that injustice must not prevail.

Afterward everyone stayed to discuss the matter more fully. The trial is to begin tomorrow. Grandfather and Sarah's father explained to us that the decision may turn on whether Mister Dangerfield came to Pennsylvania before or after the Fugitive Slave Act of 1850 was passed. If it was after the act passed, then Mister Dangerfield could be returned to his owner under that law.

There is great emotion here in this city today. There are speeches in the city parks. The entire city is horrified that this trial could return a runaway slave to a slave owner in a slave state. It seems against all good conscience to even think of such a thing. People here have become used to Negroes being free.

There is some talk of trying to raise funds for his purchase if all else fails. They say he would go for around $1,500. Oh, dearest Father and Mother, I do not understand this trafficking in men, women, and children. How can one person purchase another person? It seems to me this is against God's order.

Sarah's mother told us that we must be prepared for our bazaar to free Tookie to turn into a fair to raise money for Daniel Dangerfield instead. I want Mister Dangerfield to be free, I truly do. But I also want Pearl's sister to be free. Must one be sacrificed for the other? I know Sarah's mother is right. How can we have a bazaar in just three days to raise money for purchasing a slave (our Tookie) and ignore the needs of this man who is on trial for his life tomorrow? Yet it hurts. I wish there were a way for both to be free. Sarah and I prayed together tonight for God's mercy and justice to prevail in the trial tomorrow.

With trust in God,

Hannah

P.S. Grandfather and Sarah's father just came in. Grandfather sends you his love. They have decided to attend the trial and take Sarah and me with them! We will get up very early tomorrow, as many people will want to be there to support Mister Dangerfield.

Philadelphia, Pennsylvania

Fourth Month 7, 1859

Dear Father and Mother,

When we arrived, there were hundreds of Negroes at the courthouse. Marshal Yost swore in fifty special marshals ready for any emergency. Yet Grandfather told me even Marshal Yost disagrees with this arrest. Marshal Yost offered $50 toward the purchase amount and up to $200 if necessary. The hearing lasted all night. It began at four o'clock yesterday afternoon and was not over until six o'clock this morning. Yet neither Sarah nor I are tired.

There were lawyers for both sides and lots of witnesses. Some said they knew Daniel as a boy and as a young man in Loudoun. Dr. Francis Lucketts testified that he had treated Daniel for typhoid when he was the slave of the Simpsons. There were witnesses for Daniel Dangerfield as well. Grandfather told me that this was the first case for this judge since he became a U.S. commissioner.

Mother, you will never guess who I met yesterday. Sarah's father introduced me to Friend Lucretia Mott. She was there for the entire trial. She sat right next to Daniel

Dangerfield, and when the attorneys requested that she be removed, she threw her arms around Mister Dangerfield's neck and said she would rather give $100 to rescue him than one cent to purchase him. A court officer removed Friend Lucretia Mott from beside Mister Dangerfield and asked her to sit in the back of the courtroom. Mother, the attorneys for Mister Dangerfield moved her chair back so it was again next to Mister Dangerfield, and that is where she sat the entire trial. She never left his side.

At a break in the proceedings, Sarah's father, who knows Lucretia Mott from the committee work here in Philadelphia, introduced her to us. She said, "So these are the young girls who are behind the fair to raise funds to rescue young Talitha. I am pleased to meet you, dear children. There is much you can learn here today about the power of righteousness."

I asked, "Do you know Mister Dangerfield?"

Friend Lucretia Mott replied, "I know many Mister Dangerfields, Hannah. I understand you have met some yourself recently, in the blessed father and daughter God sent your way. Never underestimate the power of a yielded heart, dear Hannah. When you are willing, the Lord will send those to you who need your help."

Grandfather said he was glad to see her again, and Friend Lucretia said, "It is I who am benefited by being with you again. I have heard much of your recent efforts from Friend Samuel Janney since last I saw you. It is not easy to live in a slave state among slave owners and still speak out for justice. May God continue to bless your efforts."

Mother, I cannot describe her. She is so strong of character and of the light of Christ that her whole body reflects it. She sat with Mister Dangerfield as though never tired, no matter how long the trial was going. She sat with her knitting in her lap, her needles clicking away, and all the time staring at Commissioner Longstreth as if she were willing him to make the right decision. She told Grandfather that sometimes old ladies with knitting needles prick the consciences of judges.

She explained that she had arrived early for the hearing and gathered with several women from the antislavery society in the basement under the courtroom at Fifth and Chestnut Streets. There she saw Commissioner Longstreth sitting at a table, writing. Since she knew him to be of Quaker descent, she boldly spoke to him in the earnest hope that his conscience would not allow him to send this poor man into slavery. He was quite civil but replied that he was bound by his oath of office and must judge fairly. Nonetheless, Mother, I am certain it was her presence in that courtroom that reminded Commissioner Longstreth of a higher duty. She radiated the love of Christ as she faithfully stayed by Mister Dangerfield. It came as no surprise to many when the commissioner issued his order. He said that based on some conflicting testimony, he could not say that this Daniel Dangerfield was the same man who had fled Loudoun County years ago.

The streets were lively with both celebration and outrage. There must have been a thousand Negroes and abolitionists in the streets, rejoicing in the decision to release

Mister Dangerfield. But there were an equal number of southern sympathizers, who were furious at Mister Dangerfield's release. Due to some quick thinking by several Quaker boys not much older than I, Mister Dangerfield was led to safety. The boys escorted another man, who resembled Mister Dangerfield, to a carriage and drove him off, while the real Dangerfield was spirited away in the company of friends.

Mother, I have been forever changed by today's events.

Your humble daughter,

Hannah

Philadelphia, Pennsylvania

Fourth Month 8, 1859

Dearest Father and Mother,

It is very late, but I cannot rest until I recount every moment of this most momentous day.

We have slept little the last few days, between the trial and readying the goods for the bazaar. Sarah's mother has worked tirelessly. We owe her so much. She received, cataloged, and arranged all the goods for sale. Others from the sewing circle were there to assist, but it was Sarah's mother who gave of her heart and soul all day. The fair was to begin at ten o'clock. We were at the auditorium by seven to arrange the tables and place cloths over each one. We tagged and displayed the goods as Sarah's mother suggested. She has such a flair for display, Mother. I do so wish you could have been here with us.

The fair opened with great excitement. Everyone there was still full of the joy of the victory in Commissioner Longstreth's court. There was much to celebrate and the people were in a very generous mood. Often if an item had a price of five dollars, a buyer would give us seven. Or if the asking price for an item was ten dollars, a buyer might give us twenty. It was astonishing to Sarah and me. Many people I was just meeting for the first time wanted to know all about Pearl and Talitha.

Lucretia Mott stopped by and selected a purse that Sarah had made. Sarah was thrilled and wanted to give it to her. Friend Lucretia clucked her tongue and said, "Dear Friend Sarah, you would give me this gift from your heart, but we must both give Talitha a gift by the exchange—you with your beautiful stitchery and me with my coins. Together we will help set her free." Sarah said she felt as if she were dancing on air. Of course, I know that we Quakers do not dance, but sometimes we feel like it.

Then Friend Lucretia took me by the hand and led me to a small stage. I was unprepared for what happened next. Friend Lucretia, the little woman with the big voice, got the attention of the crowd. All the bazaar activity stopped and a hush fell over the room. Friend Lucretia introduced me as the young lady who was teaching Pearl to read and write. Everyone applauded. Friend Lucretia pushed me gently in front of her and said, "Hannah Brown has a few words to say about Pearl and her sister, Talitha, for whom we will buy many items today at this bazaar. Hannah?"

Mother, I looked out over the crowd. Everyone was staring at me, waiting for me to speak. My mouth was dry and my hands were damp. My heart was racing. Friend Lucretia whispered in my ear, "Just tell them Pearl's story." I found Sarah in the crowd. She gave me a smile of encouragement. *If I pretend I am telling my story to Sarah only, I will be all right,* I thought. And so I began "Pearl is about my age. I cannot tell you exactly how old she is, for she does not know. Her father, Joseph, loved his wife, Charity, very much. They had three children: Pearl, William, and Talitha. Pearl's brother was sold a few years ago and Pearl's family does not know where he is now. Charity's heart was broken when William was sold. She got swamp fever and she did not have the strength to live. She died, and the little baby she was carrying inside her died, too. Joseph decided to run away from this South Carolina plantation with his two daughters. Pearl calls him Pappy. He is a strong man; some of you met him a few months ago. He wants nothing more than for his family to be together in Freedom Land. That's what he calls Canada. When Pearl first came to our home, she was very frightened. She wouldn't even speak. Mother and I are helping her learn to read and write. The only time Pearl was ever whipped was when the master of the plantation thought she was trying to learn to read. When Pearl's mammy died (that's what she called her mother), the master took Talitha to the big house. He makes her stay awake all night to watch over their baby at the foot of the bed that he and the mistress sleep in. He thinks that if he keeps Talitha (Pearl calls her Tookie), then Joseph will come back for her, and he can capture Joseph.

"Pearl is very worried about her father. She knows he will not be able to live in freedom knowing that his daughter,

Talitha, the last living child he had with their mother, is still in slavery. Pearl is very anxious to join her father, but she cries a lot for her sister. She loves her very much. Thank you all so much for what you are doing here today to raise money to purchase Talitha."

As the audience applauded, Friend Lucretia came forward again and placed her hand on my shoulder. "Do you know what *Talitha* means, Hannah?" I shook my head. "One day a long time ago, a man named Jairus saw Jesus. He fell at his feet and pleaded with him, saying, 'My little daughter is at the point of death; please come and lay your hands on her, that she may get well and live.' Jesus went with Jairus to his house, but on their way, some people met them with the bad news that Jairus's daughter had died. They told Jairus not to trouble Jesus anymore. But Jesus, overhearing what was being spoken, said to the man, 'Do not be afraid any longer, only believe.' When Jesus came to the child's home, he took the child by the hand and said to her, '*Talitha cumi!*' which means, 'Little girl, I say to you, arise!' And immediately the girl got up and began to walk.

"'Little girl, arise!' That is what Jesus said to Jairus's daughter, and that is what we ask him to say to Talitha now. May the Lord work in a mighty way to set her free from her chains, not of death but of bondage. We all agree with Jesus and say together, '*Talitha cumi!*'"

The audience broke out in applause and cheers. Everyone was so moved by the preaching of Friend Lucretia Mott. My spirit soared, Mother. I cannot remember a time when my heart felt as though it would break from joy. Sarah and I hugged and I just knew in my spirit that little Tookie—Talitha—would one day be set free. I thought my heart could not contain my joy, but at the end of the fair we had collected $1,327, more than enough to pay for her purchase. Sarah and I jumped up and down until Sarah's mother had to remind us we were young ladies! Yet I could tell she was just as happy as we.

Grandfather and Sarah's father arrived to help us close up our shop and put away the tables. They had another surprise. They took us to a very large antislavery meeting at Samson Hall that night to celebrate Daniel Dangerfield's release. Robert Purvis was there. So was Lucretia Mott. Many members of the committee were there. Grandfather pointed out to me these notable men and women. I felt as if I were in the presence of angels. Father, there were also some very rude southerners present. They created such a disturbance by stamping, hallooing, groaning, and hollering, that it was impossible to hear the speakers. The society president's efforts to preserve order were in vain. At one point the hecklers rushed forward toward the speakers at the podium. Grandfather held Sarah and me close to him. I don't know whether I was excited or fearful; my emotions have been in such a whirlwind for the last few days. At last the police arrived and arrested some of the disturbers.

We did not come back to the Smiths' house until very late. I could not rest, though, until I had written to you. We

are tired but very happy. Grandfather will finish his publishing and nursery business in the next few days, and then
we will leave. Sarah and I will rest tomorrow but, dear
Mother, you will be pleased to know that Sarah and I plan to
work diligently on our quilt for the rest of the time I am here.

With fondest love,

Hannah

Philadelphia, Pennsylvania

Fourth Month 10, 1859

Dearest Father and Mother,

Tonight Grandfather and Sarah's father attended a committee meeting about Pearl and Talitha. Another appeal is going out to Master Worthy this week for the purchase of Talitha for $1,300. Surely, he cannot turn down such a handsome amount for a young child.

Grandfather told us there are rumors of warrants out for the rearrest of Daniel Dangerfield. Poor man! There will be no rest for his weary feet nearer than the free soil of Canada. He is being guarded by the committee but will soon be on his way. Maybe he will meet Joseph.

Now, Mother, examine this quilt square carefully. See the tiny even stitches. You should be pleased. My stitchery is getting so much better. Perhaps I will be ready for marriage one day after all. If you see Joshua, tell him Grandfather and I will return soon. Sarah's Uncle Robert may publish the map that he and Grandfather have been working on. He and his partner, Thomas Reynolds, are quite pleased with the sales of Grandfather's previous map of Loudoun County. It has sold well, even at their store here in Philadelphia. I suppose the ties between the Quakers in Bucks County, Pennsylvania, and those in Loudoun County, Virginia, have helped the sales.

We leave in two days. I will see you soon.

Forever your obedient daughter,

Hannah

Goose Creek, Virginia

Fourth Month 17, 1859

Dear Sarah,

It has been calm since we returned. I think that is a good thing. I've had quite enough excitement in my life in the last month. Grandfather and I spend most of our afternoons in the garden. I rush home from school to help. Nothing brings me more pleasure in life than digging my hands in the rich earth. Joshua stopped by today. He said he missed seeing me while I was in Philadelphia.

I didn't tell him everything, as I am still not sure where he stands on the issue of slavery. He asked about the Dangerfield trial, as he had heard from Uncle Richard that we were there. The local papers here, both the *Washingtonian* and the *Democratic Mirror,* printed much of the testimony of the witnesses, so Joshua knew quite a bit about it. The newspapers even spoke about Lucretia Mott, but they did not tell the whole story. You should have seen Joshua's face when I described Friend Lucretia with her knitting needles clicking and clacking as a constant reminder to Commissioner Longstreth that he should do the right thing.

Sarah, I was surprised how much I missed spending time with Pearl. Mother brought her back to the attic room while we were gone. I told Pearl the whole story about Daniel Dangerfield. Pearl is quite funny now that she is willing to talk. At the plantation, the overseer would blow the horn for them to wake up, blow the horn for them to come to the field, blow the horn for a meal break, and blow the horn for them to stop working. She imitated what the overseer looks like when he blows the horn. You should have seen her, Sarah. Her eyes bugged out and her cheeks filled with air while she made strange trumpeting sounds in her throat. I kept telling her to hush, but I was laughing so hard. I am surprised no one found us.

Today she told me about Christmas Day on her plantation. She is surprised we Quakers do not value Christmas Day any more than any other First Day. At the plantation there is much preparation for the Christmas celebrations. Holiday festivities last from the week before Christmas until New Year's Day. The master and mistress have banquets and dances. Pearl said the best thing about it all was the extra ration of fruits or sweets the slaves would get on Christmas Day. Once there was such a grand party in the big house that Pearl was told to help the house servants.

When she first came into the kitchen and saw the mince pies, the apple pies, and the cakes lining the pantry shelves, she stood for fifteen minutes without moving. The house servants carried in legs of mutton and venison and long links of sausages. Bowls of eggnog were filled high with thick cream and sprinkled with spices. The sights and smells overwhelmed her until the slave in charge of the kitchen told Pearl she had better get on her apron and help out before she sent her out to the fields. Pearl said that a tall green cedar tree reached the ceiling of the entrance hall. The tree was decorated with ropes of colored paper circled together into chains, and garlands of popcorn and berries. The tree had lighted candles made on the plantation from the wax of marsh myrtle berries. Her eyes sparkled as she told me about it.

She said that Christmas for the slaves was very different. They did not have to work on Christmas Day. The slaves managed to have their parties, too. After the praise gatherings where they worshiped together, they would have a picnic by the river. Pearl said that the reason why she and her pappy were able to survive in the swamp when they were on the run through North Carolina and southern Virginia was that they knew how to fish. An Edisto River slave knows the rivers, creeks, marshes, and backwaters, and no one ties as strong a fishing net as a slave. Crabs, clams, and oysters were Christmas dinner, along with a captured rabbit or possum. But oh, how Pearl wanted to taste that mutton, drink a cup of eggnog, and finish her meal with some spicy mince pie. They would dance and sing until late at night. Their party did not sound as fancy as the one in the big house, but I imagine it must have been more fun.

The doctor has pronounced Pearl fit to travel, and I told her it would soon be time for her to continue on her journey and join her father. I will miss her. Doctor Janney told me he heard that Mister Blockett is back in town. The name of that man sends shivers down my spine. If I never see him again, that will be too soon.

Your devoted friend missing you
every day more and more,

Hannah

Philadelphia, Pennsylvania

Fourth Month 24, 1859

Dear Hannah,

Mother and I went to another Antislavery Society meeting, and I talked with Charlotte Forten. Do you remember her uncle, Robert Purvis, a key member of the committee, whom you met when you stayed with us before? Daniel Dangerfield stayed with her family after the celebration of the eighth of this month. She told me that Mister Dangerfield is no longer residing with them, and she has learned that he is now safe in Canada. I knew you would want to know.

I miss you, dear friend. No word yet on Tookie. I will let you know as soon as we hear.

Your devoted friend,

Sarah

Philadelphia, Pennsylvania

Fourth Month 28, 1859

Dear Hannah,

We got word tonight that Master Worthy might be willing to sell Talitha, but the price is now $1,500. The committee is concerned with setting a precedent. Father explained that this is an exorbitant price and if it is paid, the work of the committee, which has limited funds, will be made more difficult.

I know you will be discouraged. Do not be faint of heart, though. The Lord will show us a way.

Your friend,

Sarah

Goose Creek, Virginia

Fourth Month 30, 1859

Dear Sarah,

Tonight Grandfather, Father, Mother, and I met to discuss the plan of the committee. Grandfather is to take Pearl with him to Philadelphia, disguised in Quaker dress. The large bonnet will hide her face, and if he takes the back roads, he will likely avoid controversy and discovery. Once in Philadelphia, Pearl will be turned over to others to continue her journey up the Liberty Line. I hope you will meet Pearl when she comes to your city.

I begged Grandfather to let me go, too, but he says it is much too dangerous. The dog patrols have increased to almost nightly in this area. The sheriff is concerned that the news of Daniel Dangerfield's successful trial, as he is an escaped slave from our very own county, will urge other slaves to run away from here as well. The slave owners nearby have been meeting to discuss what they can do to stop the flood of runaways from crossing the river. Grandfather says the borders will be especially well guarded. He said he leaves tomorrow night with Pearl.

I helped Father ready the wagon for their journey. I guess I shouldn't have been surprised when I saw a false floor in the bed of the wagon. If necessary, Grandfather can hide Pearl under the wagon flooring. What a horrible place to ride! A wagon ride while sitting on the buckboard on these back roads shakes one to the bones as it is. I tried to make the false space as comfortable for Pearl as possible, just in case. I spread out Frank's old blanket and put some hay in a muslin cloth bag for a little pillow. Father and I readied the supplies, food, water, and of course Grandfather's maps.

I gave Pearl her last reading lesson. She is getting better, but I do not think she could hold her own if challenged. We hugged goodbye. Pearl said she would never forget the kindness of my family. I said I would never forget Pearl and that she was not to worry about Tookie. We would not stop trying to purchase her from Mister Buck Worthy. I showed her how to tie her bonnet and secure her kerchief around her shoulders. She giggled, saying that these were the finest clothes she had ever owned. I told her she looked like a fine Quaker girl, and we both laughed.

I will give Joshua this letter to post for me, as he is going to town for Uncle Richard. We have much to do tonight. Note the horrible stitches in this quilt square. Alas!

Your devoted but very busy friend,

Hannah

On the Way to Philadelphia

Fifth Month 2, 1859

Dear Sarah,

You will be amazed at the contents of this letter.

When darkness came over Evergreen, Mother and I went down to the barn with Pearl. She makes a striking Quaker girl. Mother adjusted the big bow on her bonnet and Pearl threw her arms around Mother. Mother hugged her tight. I could only think of how grateful Charity must be in heaven for my mother's arms around her daughter. Pearl and I hugged goodbye again, and Father helped her get up into the wagon to sit next to Grandfather on the buckboard. "Take good care of your *package*, Grandpappy," I whispered as he flicked the reins and the horses began to pull the wagon up the hill.

Father, Mother, and I returned to the house. Mother and I did some sewing but my heart was not in it. I helped Mother with the baby, who is just now beginning to walk. Mother asked me to go to the springhouse to bring up some milk. After I pulled up the jug of milk from the cool waters, I heard them. Dogs. Barking loudly. Coming down from North Fork. Patrols, Sarah. With Grandfather only two hours away! I knew he could not be that far. Suddenly I remembered that I had not secured the trapdoor in the barn. There had seemed no need with Pearl gone, but now I hurried to the barn to close the trapdoor. The cattle were not anywhere near the barn, and I had to get one into the barn to help disguise the scent. I chased old Bessie down from the hill and tugged on her lead to get her into the barn.

From down the hill, I saw the outline of a man with dogs at the door of our home. Father was speaking with him. It was Blockett! The dogs were going crazy now because of the fresh scent of Pearl. Blockett realized he was onto something and gave the dogs a longer lead. They tore at their leashes and raced to the barn. I was terrified and jumped up on the fence. The dogs bared their teeth and snarled and strained at their leashes. Blockett raised his kerosene lantern high and spied the fresh wagon wheel ruts in the ground. The sheriff, holding the reins of Blockett's horse, a fine chestnut stallion, caught up with Blockett at our barn, and he too saw the wagon wheel ruts. Blockett handed the dogs' lead lines to the sheriff and told him he'd be back for them later. He mounted his horse, kicked his sides, and galloped off, following the wagon tracks.

When the sheriff left with the dogs, I ran back into the house. I was crying and carrying on something awful, Sarah. I was so frightened for Grandfather and Pearl. That stallion would have no trouble catching up with Grandfather. His old plow horses pulling the weight of the wagon, even with a two-hour lead, would be no match for that muscled beast. I hated him, Sarah. I hated Blockett with everything in me.

Father tried to calm me down but I wouldn't be calmed. "Father, we have to do something to warn Grandfather."

There was a swift knock at the door. It was Joshua. His horse was tied to our fencepost. "Friend Thomas Brown, I know all about it. I have known for months." I must have looked shocked, for he said to me, "Your Grandfather placed his faith in me." Then he turned to Father and said, "Now I ask you, sir, to place your faith in me as well. I was returning from town when I saw Friend Yardley. I shouted a hello to him. He tipped his hat in my direction, but the Quaker girl riding beside him did not so much as wave at me. Then when I heard the dog patrols, I came here immediately. When I saw Hannah, I knew that the young lady with Friend Yardley was not your daughter." Then Joshua turned to me and said, "Hannah, you do not like your bonnet. I knew that if you were with your Grandfather, you would not have your head covered. The man who flew away from here on the mighty stallion—I assume he is after Friend Yardley and his charge?"

"Yes," said Father. "He is a slave catcher from South Carolina."

"Then you must trust me. I have a plan but there is no time to waste. I am fond of Friend Yardley and do not want to see him arrested. But there is only one aspect of my plan to which you must agree—Hannah must ride with me."

"Me ride with you!"

Joshua explained to Father, "The wagon will slow Friend Yardley down significantly. The slave catcher on that fine horse should be able to catch him, but if I can get there first, . . ."

Father asked, "However will you do that, Joshua?"

"Friend Yardley has not only taught me to survey the roads, but he has taught me the roads himself. Those many days of journeying with him have paid off. He showed me a shortcut to the river. It is not one that the slave catcher will know, as he will be following the wagon tracks and keeping to ordinary roads. I am sure Blockett knew a quick way to the river, but it is the quick way by regular road. Friend Yardley taught me about paths many do not know, which he has used for his activities through the years."

Father looked at Mother and she nodded her head.

"We must hurry. There is no time to waste," said Joshua and untied his horse and mounted him.

Father gave me a leg up onto Joshua's horse, and Mother grabbed one of my bonnets and gave it to me. "You may need this," was all that she said. There was no time for goodbyes as Joshua kicked Lightning into a gallop. Lightning was true to his name, and I clung tightly to Joshua as we rode swiftly through the night.

Joshua leaned low in the saddle, urging Lightning to go faster and faster. We rode through unkempt paths where I ducked my head behind Joshua to try to avoid the branches as they whipped by. We rode through creeks. We rode and rode and rode—hard and fast. A few miles before the river, we caught up with Grandfather's wagon. Joshua helped me down and up into the wagon. I held the reins of the horses while Grandfather helped Pearl up onto Lightning, behind Joshua. They took off down a darkened path.

I barely had time to tie my bonnet in place before Blockett reined in his stallion, soapy with sweat from a fast gallop, right next to our wagon. My heart, which started beating fast in the springhouse, was racing now. I kept my head down. Grandfather had told me that he would do all the talking, and for that I was grateful.

Blockett raised his pistol and shouted at Grandfather, "Halt!" Grandfather whoaed the horses to a stop and turned to Blockett. "Where are you going?" barked Blockett. "And who is that there with you?"

Grandfather said, "What authority have you to brandish your weapon like that?"

Blockett replied, "I have a warrant from the sheriff's office for the capture and arrest of two slaves, one of whom you have there with you."

Grandfather said, "Man, you will scare my granddaughter with all these theatrics. Put down your gun. How dare you! Who are you to threaten me with lies and accusations? Don't you have more important business to attend to?"

"You are my business," replied Blockett. His voice made my skin grow cold. "You and that supposed granddaughter there. You, girl—show your face."

Grandfather spoke gently to me. I was shaking. "Do not answer this man's commands. He is not your father nor your grandfather." I leaned in closer to Grandfather. He seemed so calm and confident. I was sure Blockett could hear my heart beating. Then, turning to the slave catcher Blockett, Grandfather said sternly, "You show your face first."

Blockett lifted his lantern and the light glowed on his wizened face. I shuddered as I stole a glance at him from under the brim of my bonnet. "Ah, Mister Blockett, I presume. I have heard a lot about you but have not had the pleasure of meeting you. I understand you have visited with my family, though. Mister Blockett, the persons whom you seek are not with me. Why don't you trouble some other poor soul and leave me and my granddaughter alone. We have many miles to keep until we will be at our friends home in Waterford by her bedtime."

"That is not your granddaughter!" Blockett bellowed. At that he kicked his horse, rode near my side of the wagon, and snatched at my bonnet, which was tied securely under my chin. I lurched in fear away from Blockett and leaned as close to Grandfather as I could.

"If you dare lay a hand on my granddaughter again, I will wallop you good, gun or no gun. We Quakers are a peace-loving people, but I will not stand for any harm to come to my granddaughter." Grandfather then turned to me and said, "Please remove your bonnet and speak to this poor excuse for a man. Tell him your name."

With trembling hands I untied my bonnet. My hair, which had been pinned up before my ride on Lightning, fell around my shoulders. Blockett's lantern shone in my eyes as I said firmly, "I am Hannah Maria Brown, daughter of Thomas and Elizabeth Brown, and granddaughter of Yardley Taylor."

Blockett was stunned. He turned his horse and headed off.

Grandfather and Joshua had arranged to meet at a little-known path close to a creek near Edward's Ferry. I was never so happy to see someone as when I saw Joshua and Pearl standing by Lightning. Tonight Grandfather plans to take his wagon across the Potomac River by ferry, because a certain ferryman is on duty. The man is a friend to the Friends on the Underground Railroad. Joshua and Grandfather spoke quietly together while I told Pearl what had happened. Then Grandfather told me that I must come with him to Philadelphia. It would not do for Blockett to return to Evergreen tomorrow to find me there. Also, Joshua said it was too dangerous for Pearl to ride up front on the buckboard, with Blockett on their trail. I could help Grandfather hide Pearl away when necessary.

"I will tell your mother and father that you are safe and all is well," said Joshua.

I looked at Grandfather and asked, "Won't Mother and Father disapprove? After all, they think I am only going to the river with Joshua."

"I almost forgot," said Joshua and pulled a bundle from his saddle bag. "Your mother gave me a bundle and said, 'It's for Hannah—for her trip.'"

I untied the string around the cloth bundle. There was a slate, chalk, and the composition book.

"We can continue our lessons!" said Pearl.

I smiled as I realized that Mother knew all along what might happen. Grandfather shook Joshua's hand. "You will make a fine surveyor one day. You know the hills and hideaways as well as I do."

Joshua mounted Lightning and said to me, "I will expect some apple pie when next I see you." I felt myself blush. He winked at Grandfather and turned Lightning and raced back toward Goose Creek.

Grandfather, Pearl, and I arranged ourselves in the wagon and headed for the ferry just another mile away. We all got a good laugh when we told Pearl about Blockett's face when I took off my bonnet. "He was expecting a black face for sure and certain!" declared Pearl.

When we neared the ferry, Grandfather went ahead by himself. He came back and said, "All is arranged." He helped Pearl into the secret compartment in the wagon, and we were able to cross the Potomac River into Maryland without further incident. Grandfather hurried the horses on until we reached Pennsylvania. He pulled over to let Pearl out.

"Breathe deep, young lady. Breathe the fresh air of freedom." Pearl was so excited that she gave out a whoop, jumped down from the wagon, and kissed the ground.

Soon we will be in Philadelphia. Oh, Sarah, then I will deliver this letter to you in person. Yet I think that when Grandfather tells the story, it will become somewhat embellished and all the better for the telling. I can't wait to see you. And now you will meet Pearl.

Your exhausted but grateful friend,

Hannah

Philadelphia, Pennsylvania

Fifth Month 10, 1859

Dearest Father and Mother,

All is well. Grandfather and I are having a delightful visit with the Smiths. Although our route was not our normal one, Grandfather made his delivery with nothing significant to report. I am sure Joshua told you about the earlier portion of our journey. Our package is safe, and we are engaged in discussions with those who can forward it on to its final destination. Grandfather and I are going to the nursery today and hope to purchase some new plantings for the return trip. I will write again soon, when Sarah and I finish another quilt square.

Your loving daughter,

Hannah

Philadelphia, Pennsylvania

Fifth Month 15, 1859

Dearest Father and Mother,

Mother, this quilt square is terribly stitched. I know you will shudder when you see my stitches an inch long rather than twelve per inch. I hurriedly stitched up this pocket so you could read what has happened.

The first night, Sarah's father secreted Pearl in the attic eaves in a special room. Sarah's father moved a chest in front of the small door after Sarah and I gave Pearl a blanket and some food. There has been much activity, and Sarah's father says that lately slave catchers with warrants have been able to search the homes of several families known to assist fugitives. Fortunately, no one has been captured, but he did not want to take any chances with Pearl.

The next day things were very quiet. Grandfather told Sarah's father over breakfast that Mister Blockett won't take long to figure out we're not in Virginia anymore. Grandfather fears some folks in Loudoun who aren't too happy with his abolitionist activities might suggest to Blockett they can find him in Philadelphia working with abolitionist sympathizers. Once he gets here, he will make inquiries and learn of our friendship with the Smiths. Sarah's father left to arrange the next stop for Pearl on her journey north to Canada. Sarah and I were so glad that we had the day with Pearl. We took a basket of food upstairs for her. I worked with Pearl on her reading. (I wish she were better equipped for this journey, but at least she can write her name and sound out some of the easier words. Mother, thank you for your package. I have worked with Pearl every day we have had together on this journey. She can write her name both as *Pearl* and as *Polly*. She can recognize her father's name, *Joseph,* and her sister's name, *Tookie,* when I write them for her.)

Then there was a loud, urgent knock on the front door. Sarah and I looked at one another in fright. We pushed Pearl back into the small room under the eaves and put the basket of food in with her. We shut the little door, but Sarah signaled it was too late to push the chest in front of the door. It would likely be heard. Sarah went to the doorway and listened at the top of the steps. We were all much relieved when Sarah said it was a Friend. We opened the door and told Pearl to stay there while we went to see what message he might bring regarding her passage to Canada. We moved the chest in front of the door, just in case anyone else should arrive.

When we reached the bottom of the stairs, we heard this Friend say, "Your young charge is not safe here. The committee received word that the slave catcher, Blockett, has arrived in Philadelphia and is making inquiries. He has money to buy information, and the case of Pearl is better-known here because of Hannah's speech at the bazaar. Pearl must not stay another night. Friends James and Lucretia Mott send word that it would be their supreme honor to receive Pearl into their home at Roadside and forward her on the line. Friend Lucretia remembers fondly the efforts of young Sarah and young Hannah in the cause of freedom. I will return this evening after dark for Pearl."

I went upstairs and pushed the chest aside, opened the door, and told Pearl the news that she would be staying with the Motts that night and then leave to join her father in Canada. Pearl said, "You aren't going with me?"

"No, but you can trust these Friends with your life. Do not be afraid, Pearl. They will send you from home to home among those who believe, as does Grandfather, in your God-given right to freedom. These Friends are called abolition-ists." Pearl recoiled in terror at the mention of the word abolitionist. "What's wrong, Pearl?"

"In the South we were told that abolitionists are people who will kidnap us and sell us."

"Who told you that?"

"Why, Master said it was true."

"Pearl, what Master Worthy said is anything but the truth. *Abolitionist* is a word that comes from *abolish*—it means "get rid of." These people want to get rid of slavery forever, and that is why they risk their own safety to make sure you reach freedom. Do not fear; these abolitionists are your friends."

Father, can you believe this? They spread such lies just to keep runaway slaves from finding the help they need from the very people who can give it to them. I told Pearl that I had a note in my pocket that Sarah's father had given me the night before. A note that was sent to be read to Pearl. A note brought by an abolitionist. I read the note to her:

Dear Pearl,

I am safe and in the Promised Land. This is Freedom Land, Pearl. The land of Canaan we sang about together with your mammy. There are friends who will bring you to me. I will see you soon. Then together, somehow, we will free your younger sister. Remember this: "Be strong and of good courage; be not afraid, neither be thou dismayed: for the LORD thy God is with thee wheresoever thou goest."

Pappy

"Pappy's in Canada?" Pearl said, her eyes brimming with tears.

"Yes, and he has sent you a message that you can keep in your pocket. I know you cannot read it, Pearl, but I will read it to you over and over until you leave tonight, so you can memorize it. It will comfort you in the night when you are afraid."

That night, after dark, a Friend came to take Pearl to the Mott's farm. Grandfather and Sarah's father explained to us what the committee had planned for Pearl. She would be sent from farm to farm along the Liberty Line, from Philadelphia to Bristol to Bensalem to Quakertown to Doylestown to Buckingham to New Hope and across the Delaware River to Lambertville, New Jersey. After that, the most dangerous part of her journey would begin. She would be taken from Trenton to Jersey City to Newark to New York. There were many spies in that area of New Jersey, as well as some proslavery sympathizers. More importantly, the slave hunters' headquarters is in New Brunswick, on the way. I asked Sarah's father why they would send Pearl by that route if it is so dangerous. He told us that it is still the fastest route to New York City, and then the train will take her directly to Rochester and on to Canada. With Blockett hot on the trail and a bounty on her head, the faster they move this package to its final destination, the better.

The next morning, Sarah and I insisted on seeing Pearl again before she left. Sarah's father took us in the buggy to Roadside. I gave Pearl one more reading lesson, Mother, and wished I had time for more. I do not know why I sense such urgency in this matter. Yet, like you, Mother, I am trying to learn to pay attention to these urges of the Spirit.

Friend Lucretia poured tea for us, and for just a few moments Sarah, Pearl, and I were like cousins with no worries. We laughed and talked and had a most marvelous time. Sarah talked with Friend Lucretia about the plan to purchase Tookie. Friend Lucretia says that she knows Reverend Grimes of the Twelfth Street Baptist Church in Boston. He used to live in Loudoun County, Virginia, and has raised funds before for the purchase of slaves. She will write to him immediately.

When it was time to say goodbye, Sarah and I gave Pearl our presents. Sarah had made her an impressive disguise. We made her try it on. With her hair tucked under the cap, she looked like a Quaker boy. I taught her to hook her thumbs in her britches and swagger as I have seen Joshua do. We all laughed. I gave Pearl a bundle that held her slate and chalk and composition book. It was hard to say goodbye. Pearl has become like a dear sister. Friend Lucretia led us in a time of silent prayer for Pearl and her journey.

After this wondrous visit we returned to Sarah's home. Grandfather began to discuss how to send me back to Virginia. Grandfather had hoped to meet with Sarah's uncle, but he is on a project in New York City that will last several months. He is working on a map of New York. You can imagine how that piqued Grandfather's curiosity. He determined that he would travel on to New York City to meet with him. Grandfather said it might be advantageous for him to be in New York to verify that Pearl made it safely to that part of her journey.

Well, Mother, you know I am your father's granddaughter. It was all I could do to persuade him to let me go with him. "Grandfather, I must know Pearl is safe. Cannot I go with you to New York City? Then I can be sure she is almost to her destination." When Grandfather protested that he might have to help Mister Smith with his work, I reminded him that I was an excellent note taker and could assist in many ways. Finally Grandfather relented and is taking me with him. We leave by train tomorrow.

Your adventurous daughter,

Hannah

Philadelphia, Pennsylvania

Fifth Month 17, 1859

Dear Hannah,

I am writing to you in care of my uncle. No sooner had you left on the train than we received distressing news from the committee about Tookie. They have heard from Buck Worthy, master of the Oakwood Plantation. He has changed his mind and doubled the price for Tookie. He wants $3,000. I will work tirelessly, Hannah, to raise these funds. Mother is helping me with another bazaar. However, the committee says that a direct sale is not likely. It cannot pay such outrageous prices.

It was a blessing and a joy to be with you, my dearest friend. I am most hopeful that you and your grandfather will stop here again on your return from New York City.

Your friend,

Sarah

New York City

Fifth Month 21, 1859

Dear Sarah,

Dearest friend, do not be discouraged or weary of doing well. Your efforts will not be in vain. You are on the side of truth and freedom. You are on the Lord's side. I wish I could be there to help you raise the funds. However, I do have something I want to send to you. Look deep inside the pocket of this quilt square. There is a pearl that Grandfather once gave to me for purity of heart. I can think of nothing I would rather do than give it to you. Please ask your father to sell it and give the proceeds to the fund to purchase Tookie. I have spoken with Grandfather about this. His eyes welled up with tears, and at first I thought he was disappointed with me. Then he lifted me up and twirled me around and kissed me on the cheek. "You have sold the pearl of great value for something of even greater value. You have made me glad, Hannah Maria Brown!"

Grandfather and your uncle are hunched over drawing boards and maps all day. Grandfather is quite intrigued with the latest equipment your uncle has for surveying. I am finding the days long as I wait for word of Pearl. I say prayers for her safety and protection throughout the day. Yet I yearn to hear word from her. The committee knows we are staying here and will forward word to us as soon as they know anything.

I know that Quakers do not read fanciful novels. Yet I found a book in the library that astonishes me. Grandfather has given me permission to read it. It is called *Uncle Tom's Cabin,* and it is a story that reminds me of Joseph and Pearl. My heart is so burdened for Pearl and Tookie as I read it. We simply must find a way for this family to be together again in freedom. I will not rest until we see safely Joseph and his daughters reunited in Canada.

Affectionately,

Hannah

Philadelphia, Pennsylvania

Fifth Month 23, 1859

Dear Hannah,

I did not think the news could be worse. We have been working tirelessly here to prepare for the bazaar to raise the double price for Tookie. Today, however, Friend Lucretia stopped by with a letter from Reverend Grimes. He had attempted to secure the purchase of Tookie through an abolitionist posing as a slave owner, in the hopes that the price would be more reasonable. This man inquired several times of plantation owners in the area about young house servant girls for sale. He inquired specifically of Buck Worthy but he refuses to sell Tookie. The abolitionist made several offers, raising each by several hundred dollars, but each time he was refused. Reverend Grimes fears that he will refuse to sell her at any price.

Hannah, there must be a way.

Your devoted friend,

Sarah

Rochester, New York

Sixth Month 5, 1859

Dear Sarah,

Mother would be horrified to see this quilt square. It must never be in our friendship quilt! It is even worse than the one I sent to her. Perhaps it should serve as a model for all young Quaker girls of how *not* to stitch. I made this square in record time to get this news to you. The pocket is stuffed with pages, as I have so much to tell you. I am in Rochester, New York! Now let me tell you how I got here.

We had been in New York City for about two weeks when one day Grandfather said he was taking me to lunch at Downing's Oyster House on the corner of Broad and Wall Streets. No sooner had our oyster stew arrived than a man came to our table and said mysteriously to Grandfather that his package had arrived and would be waiting for him downstairs. We finished our stew and rose to leave. Instead of exiting the restaurant normally, however, Grandfather directed me down a passage past the kitchen to steps leading to the cellar. At the bottom of the steps there was a small room. Grandfather opened the door and Pearl was standing before me, dressed in your disguise. We jumped up and down with joy. All the while Grandfather was shushing us. Grandfather told me he had to discuss some matters with the Friend who had brought the message, and he would leave us to talk. Oh my goodness, Sarah, did Pearl have a lot to tell me. Her journey was perilous and exciting.

All was well for the first part of her trip. She was moved at night between homes, which were about ten or so miles apart. She stayed in barns, cellars, attics, and even one night in a hay shock in a field. She was passed from family to family in the cloak of darkest night and rested during the day, until she reached New Jersey. The next step was for her to go with a gentleman Friend of the Underground Railroad who would assist her across the Raritan River on the train and on to New York City. Just before they neared the overpass, word reached this Friend that Blockett and the other slave catchers were looking for Pearl at the station. Master Buck Worthy had increased the bounty again for her return, and there were flyers with her description at the station. The Friend told Pearl they must go by boat instead.

When Pearl showed him the disguise you sewed for her, the Friend was delighted. Pearl quickly changed her clothes behind a tree. Then this Friend showed her how to walk like a boy. "Walk heavy, there, young girl! Lift up your head. Eyes straight ahead. Walk straight and heavy now." You would have been proud to see Pearl in the disguise you made for her. With those clothes and her new way of walking, no one would have thought she was a girl. They were able to evade the slave catcher and make their way by boat to Perth Amboy and on to New York City.

When Grandfather returned, he was with an elder Friend named Mordecai Shoemaker and his wife, Lydia. They planned to take Pearl by the New York Central Railroad from Forty-second Street Station to Rochester. There she would be safely transported across the bridge to Canada at Niagara Falls. Friends would make sure Pearl made it to Canada. I helped Pearl change into the Quaker dress Friend Lydia had brought with her for Pearl. She tried to give me back the slate and book, but I assured her those were hers to keep. I told her of our plan to purchase Tookie. I did not tell her of the discouraging news that the price had doubled, however, or that Master Worthy seemed intent on keeping her. Grandfather hurried us along, as it was imperative that Pearl not miss the train. I begged Grandfather to let us accompany Friend Mordecai and Friend Lydia to Forty-second Street Station, and he agreed. I think he was as anxious as I was to see Pearl safely on the train.

At the station, however, Grandfather spotted that evil Blockett. He did not see us while Grandfather hurried us along to another track. This put a long train between the slave catcher and us. The sight of Blockett made my skin grow cold and it also made me angry. I knew then that I had to go with Pearl—to protect her. I remembered how Blockett yanked at my bonnet when he thought I was Pearl. He would have yanked off my head, given the chance. He would be no kinder to Pearl if he had her in his grip.

I turned to Grandfather and Friend Mordecai. "I know it is your plan to take Pearl with you to Rochester, but you might as well hand Pearl over to the slave catcher if he sees you together. What is a kindly Quaker couple doing with a young Negro girl? The slave catcher will be most suspicious. If, however, Friend Lydia and I accompany Pearl, it will be as natural as can be—just a Quaker teacher and her pupils on a trip to the Falls."

Grandfather stooped to pick up a flyer on the floor of the train track. It was a reward for the capture of three slaves, including a young girl fitting Pearl's description. He looked at me for several minutes that felt like hours. Friend Mordecai touched Grandfather's arm and said, "The child is right. We may be better suited to divert Mister Blockett and keep him from boarding the train." Grandfather crumpled up the flyer in his hand, hugged me, and told me he would take the next train to Rochester. Friend Mordecai gave the three tickets to his wife and we quickly boarded the train. I had the utmost confidence that if anyone could divert Mister Blockett, it would be Grandfather, and even though Pearl was trembling in the seat next to me, I was certain we were safe now.

How wrong I was. The train chugged out of the city. When the conductor came for our tickets, he looked curiously at the three of us. Friend Lydia calmly gave him the tickets and said, "This one is for me, and these two are for my students." The conductor tipped his hat to Friend Lydia and moved on down the train.

All was well for the first hour. Then the car door opened and a man with a small valise took a seat facing us, a few rows away. He took out some papers from the valise and read through them. He kept looking at his papers, then at Pearl, then at the papers again. Pearl noticed and nudged me. Friend Lydia pulled out her Bible and began to read. That gave me an idea. I said rather loudly, "Friend Lydia, is it time for our lessons?" Friend Lydia, who had not noticed this man, appeared a bit confused. "I thought Polly and I could do some copy work if you will lend us your Bible." I nudged Pearl, who pulled out her slate and chalk from her small bag. Pearl wrote the name *Polly* across the top of the slate. At that moment I was so thankful that Mother had insisted I teach Pearl her alphabet during the months at Evergreen. Even though reading was coming along slowly, Pearl could write her letters. If she could just copy down what she saw in the Bible, that would be enough.

The man continued to stare at us. Finally he stood and walked up to our seats. He directed his comments to Friend Lydia. "Are you a teacher?"

"Why, yes sir," replied Friend Lydia.

"And these are your students?"

"Yes. This is Hannah and this is—"

"Polly," I said quickly. I was so afraid that Friend Lydia was about to say Pearl's name.

"In the South, where I am from, it is against the law to teach reading and writing to slave children," he said coldly, looking straight at Pearl. Pearl slumped in her seat and I nudged her again hard to make her sit up straight.

"I have heard that is true," replied Friend Lydia, "but fortunately, in the fellowship of Friends we believe all should learn to read and write."

"Can this one read?" he said, pointing to Pearl.

Friend Lydia paused, not knowing what to say. I very sweetly inquired, "Would you like to hear Polly recite from the Bible?" I took the Bible from my lap, turned to Psalm 23, and said to Pearl, "Here, Polly, this is your favorite Psalm, the one about the Lord as your shepherd." Pearl took the Bible, held it up in front of her face, and recited Psalm 23.

"Read something else," he demanded.

"We really must get back to our copy work, but if you insist. Polly, why don't you recite this passage, the one you and I discussed in our last lesson, where Jesus tells of those who are blessed." I turned to Luke 6 and gave the Bible to Pearl.

She held the Bible up high in front of her and began, "'Blessed be ye poor: for yours is the kingdom of God. Blessed are ye that hunger now: for ye shall be filled. Blessed are ye that weep now: for ye shall laugh. Blessed are ye, when men shall hate you, and when they shall separate you from their company, and shall reproach you . . . But I say unto you which hear, Love your enemies, do good to them which hate you, bless them that curse you, and pray for them which despitefully use you.'"

The man shrugged his shoulders, tucked his flyers under his arm, picked up his valise, and walked to the next car. I heard him mutter as he went by, "No slave girl from Carolina can read the word of the Lord like that."

The rest of the train ride was uneventful and we arrived safely in Rochester. Friends of Friend Lydia met us at the train station and took us to the home of the Anthony family. Friend Lucretia had made arrangements for us to stay with her friend Susan and her husband.

Sarah, the most remarkable thing happened next. We were only in the Anthonys' home for a few hours when seven more slaves arrived. One of them was a fugitive slave who helps other runaways to escape. She had six passengers with her. The woman's name is Harriet Tubman. She is a most unusual person—small in stature but physically strong. Her presence seems to fill the room, and her eyes are deep pools of the love of Jesus. She embraced Pearl and told her that she had met her father, Joseph, in the community of St. Catharine's just over Niagara Falls. She placed her hands on Pearl's shoulders, looked deeply into her eyes, and said, "I will take you to him." Pearl, weary from her long and perilous journey, began to weep. Then Harriet Tubman said this: "The Lord told me this morning that I would have another child of his to take to the Promised Land. Weep no more unless it is for joy. Your prayers for deliverance have been answered."

Sarah, I have never felt the Spirit so strongly as at that moment. Neither Pearl nor I could stop the flood of tears flowing down our faces. They were tears of joy and tears of revelation. We knew in our hearts that God was on the move. He had been with Pearl as she left the cotton fields of South

Carolina and tramped through the swamps of North Carolina. He had been with her through the chase to the Potomac River in Virginia, through the hand-off from Friend to Friend for miles and miles, on the boat in New Jersey, and on the train in New York. God was on the move. I know in my heart, Sarah, that he has not forgotten Tookie. God is on the move.

In awe of his power, I remain your faithful friend,

Hannah

Rochester, New York

Sixth Month 10, 1859

Dear Sarah,

    Grandfather is here in Rochester now. He is providing surveying services to your uncle for these New York counties, and I am taking notes and helping with the chain as well. I wish Joshua were here to help.

    We got word that Pearl is safely in Canada and with her father. I miss her so.

    Is there any news about Tookie?

Your friend,

Hannah

Philadelphia, Pennsylvania

Sixth Month 17, 1859

Dear Hannah,

There is much to report, but first let me respond to that wondrous answer to our prayers that you shared in your letter. That very day, I thought of Pearl as I read this in Psalm 9:9–10, 12:

> *The LORD also will be a refuge for the oppressed,*
> *A refuge in times of trouble,*
> *And they that know thy name will put their trust in thee:*
> *For thou, LORD, hast not forsaken them that seek thee. . . .*
> *He forgetteth not the cry of the humble.*

Hannah, you are right. God is on the move, and he has not forgotten Tookie's cry, either. The abolitionist posing as a slave owner continued to try to purchase Tookie, to no avail. When Master Worthy found out that Pearl had escaped Blockett again in New York City, he was furious. Apparently, two old men strong-armed Blockett into a lengthy discussion while a train to Rochester left the station. Even though we had raised the money, (the double price Master Worthy set), he would not sell Tookie. That was when God moved. God moved in the heart of this abolitionist to plan a daring escape.

Do you remember what Pearl told us about her sister— that she had to work all night and slept some during the day? That was all true. Master Worthy and his mistress made Tookie come into their bedchamber each night and stand by the cradle to rock their baby if she should awaken. The abolitionist sent word to a trusted slave at Oakwood Plantation, who told Tookie that she should slip out that night after the master and mistress fell asleep. She was to meet this slave at the creek at the back of the house, and he would take her to the abolitionist. The abolitionist would then start her on her journey to Pearl and her father in Canada. The abolitionist gave the trusted slave the slave tag your grandfather cut off Pearl's neck, with her name on it, as proof that he could be trusted.

Tookie is only six. She is not only brave but also very clever. She missed Pearl so much, she would have tried anything to be with her. Tookie knew that if she left and the baby cried, Master Worthy would awaken. Then the dogs would be after her. Earlier that night, after dinner, when Tookie was warming the baby's milk, she took some cornbread crumbs and put them in her pocket. That night, she took the cornbread crumbs and the milk left over from the baby's last meal and mashed them together. She made a thick mush, which she fed to the baby with her fingers. The baby's tummy was so full that she slept soundly. Then she found a sharp-edged rock and clenched it in her fist. Tookie waited until Master Worthy was snoring. Then she wiggled the jagged rock and determinedly sawed through the rope that bound her to the cradle and the bed. As she slipped out the door, she whispered a silent thank you to God for the jagged piece of flint and to the master who carelessly made only one loop in the knot binding her to the bell rope that night. She ran as fast as she could to the creek. There on the other side, as promised, was the abolitionist with his wagon. The baby slept the entire night through, and when Master Worthy awoke with the rising of the sun, he realized he had been bamboozled. He called for his overseer and sent him out with the dogs, but the wagon was too far ahead. It was reported that when the overseer returned empty-handed, Master Worthy stomped around and shouted that this was the third slave in a year he had lost to a railroad that cannot be seen.

By the time you receive this letter, Tookie should be in Philadelphia. They will transport her as quickly as possible to Rochester and on to Canada to join her family. We are donating the money we raised to the committee. Mother and Father said to tell you that they are very proud of you. I am, too. You took up the cause of Jesus Christ when you cared for Pearl. Hannah, today I read these words from Psalm 10:17–18:

> *Lord, thou hast heard the desire of the humble:*
> *thou wilt prepare their heart,*

thou wilt cause thine ear to hear:
To judge the fatherless and the oppressed,
that the man of the earth may no more oppress.

Until this horrible business of buying and selling human beings made in the image of God is over and done with, there will still be oppression. But at least Joseph, Tookie, and Pearl will be oppressed no more. Oh, how I would love to see Joseph's and Pearl's faces when their beloved Tookie is returned to them!

Affectionately,

Sarah

Rochester, New York

Sixth Month 25, 1859

Dear Sarah,

Your letter last received was a great encouragement to me. Our God who is on the move is full of surprises! I would never have imagined that such a young girl as Tookie could think up such a clever idea, nor that an abolitionist I don't even know would risk his life to rescue her. Your letter gave me an idea.

I showed it to Grandfather and told him that I wanted to take Tookie to Canada. I had begun my fervent list of arguments as to why this would be a wise thing to do, when Grandfather placed his finger on my lips and said, "Hush, child. You do not have to convince me of the rightness of the thing you desire. You should accompany little Talitha to Canada, and I will make the arrangements. Besides, I have never seen Niagara Falls, and our dear neighbor Samuel Janney has told me of its extraordinary beauty. It is something I should desire to see before I see God face to face. In fact, I have heard that a man will attempt to walk across the Falls on a rope next week."

We have word from the committee that Tookie is expected in Rochester within the next few days and then will take the train to Canada. Grandfather and I will travel with her from here to St. Catharine's, Canada.

Mother and Father send you their love. Mother says that when I return, it is back to baking and stitching lessons. She says she will make no comment about my quilt squares but that if this is representative of our friendship quilt, she fears we may have to start all over again. Sarah, the stitches we worked into our friendship through all we have shared together in this amazing journey will be forever the pattern of love in my heart. I will need no quilt to remember these momentous days of our work together in the Underground Railroad.

You will remain my dearest friend forever.

Faithfully,

Hannah

St. Catharine's, Ontario, Canada

Seventh Month 1, 1859

Dear Sarah,

We waited at the train station for Tookie to arrive. Grandfather sat calmly on the bench, reading his newspaper, while I paced the platform, straining to hear a whistle or see the smoke of the coming train. When the train was five minutes late, I hurried to Grandfather. "What if it is late because a slave catcher was on the train and caught Tookie?"

"Child, you must have faith," replied Grandfather. "The good Lord did not bring Tookie this far to abandon her. Now sit."

"I can't sit, Grandfather. I am too excited. This is going to be a most wondrous day."

"Yes, child, wondrous indeed!" With that Grandfather folded his newspaper, rose, took my arm, and escorted me to the edge of the platform. He leaned out over the tracks to see if the train was coming around the bend. "I must admit, Hannah Maria, that I too am very excited. I have never seen Canada or Freedom Land, as Joseph likes to call it. I have spent years on the early stops of the Underground Railroad, but I have never had the chance to see what happens to these dear people when they finally reach Canada. I want to see their faces when they know that forever they are free. I have seen the fear, the anger, and the terror in so many eyes. The good Lord is gracious to me that I may now see the joy, the peace, and the liberty that will shine in Joseph's and Pearl's eyes as they gather up little Tookie in their arms."

"And the love," I added.

"Yes, Hannah, the love of this family is strong, and you have been privileged to share in it. So what do you think of this Underground Railroad business now, dear child?"

At that moment the train whistle sounded and we saw the billowing smoke from the engine filling the sky. I grabbed Grandfather's arm and leaned out over the edge of the platform as far as I dared. "Do you see it yet, Grandfather?" My question was answered as the black locomotive chugged around the bend and headed for the station.

We scanned the passengers as they stepped down from the cars of the train. No sign of Tookie. Grandfather and I walked down the platform, looking for any sign of a young girl. There was none.

"Ho ho!" exclaimed Grandfather. "What have we here? Dear Friend Eliza!"

Sarah, it was Eliza Janney, your dear teacher from Springdale and our neighbor from Goose Creek.

"Friend Yardley!" she responded as Grandfather tipped the brim of his hat. "Hannah, so good to see you." Then Friend Eliza laughed. "I can tell from your face, it is not me you desire to see." She then turned and said, "Talitha, it is all right. These people cared for your sister, Pearl, and your father, Joseph. Come on out now from behind my skirts."

A timid but beautiful young girl shyly emerged from behind Friend Eliza.

"Tookie!" I exclaimed. At the sound of the name Pearl had given her, Tookie's face lit up with a smile. "I have so much to tell you about your sister's adventures." I took her hand and led her to a bench, where I began to tell her about the first night Pearl came to our home. I held her hands in mine and told her how happy we were to see her. I told her about you, Sarah, and all the work you had done to help her be free. I wish you had been there with me to share that moment.

Grandfather and Friend Eliza visited for a few moments before Friend Eliza continued on her journey to visit her family. She said goodbye to Tookie, who gave her a big hug. Grandfather, Tookie, and I then spent the night with Friends and boarded the train for Canada the next day. Tookie was amazed when we crossed the bridge over the Falls, but it was Grandfather who stood there at the railroad car window with tears in his eyes. "This is the Lord at his best!" he exclaimed. "He works such wonders and then lets us share in them."

Looking at Tookie and Grandfather and knowing that in a few moments we would all be reunited with Joseph and Pearl, I said, "That he does, Grandfather!"

The train slowly came to a stop at the St. Catharine's station in Ontario, Canada. Grandfather scooped Tookie up in his strong arms and held her face to the window. "Freedom

Land, Tookie. No more masters. No more slaves. Just you and your pappy and your sister in your Promised Land."

Word had gotten through from the committee to Joseph. I saw him standing on the platform with Pearl, but Tookie had not yet seen them. Grandfather, with Tookie still in his arms, stepped down onto the platform. I was right behind. He set Tookie down gently. Oh, Sarah, you should have seen that sweet girl. She ran as fast as her legs could carry her and jumped up into her father's arms. Pearl laughed and cried all at the same time. Never have I seen such joy. Grandfather and I stood arm in arm, watching them. Our hearts were so full, I thought we would burst with joy ourselves.

Then Joseph put Tookie down next to Pearl and got down on his knees. Right there on the platform. Pearl and Tookie joined him. He raised his eyes to heaven, and with tears pouring down his face, he prayed, "Jesus, thank you for bringing my child to me. Thank you for bringing us to Freedom Land one by one. Thank you for keeping us safe, and thank you for Friends who showed us the way, fed and clothed us, and gave us shelter. Thank you for my children Pearl and Tookie, and we ask your protection over William, Lord. Thank you for the years we had with their dear mother, who is with you. Now bind us together as a family in this Promised Land. Oh, Jesus, we thank you!"

Grandfather whispered to me, "Let's give them a little time together."

As we walked to a bench on the other side of the platform, I said, "Grandfather, you asked me a question a few minutes ago—you asked what I thought about this Railroad business now."

"Yes, and what do you think, dear child?"

"How soon do you think we can get another package to the Railroad?"

I will see you soon, Sarah, when we return to Virginia by way of Philadelphia. Tell your Aunt Alice that the Lord certainly did exceedingly abundantly more than I could have asked or thought.

Your committed friend,

Hannah

Quaker Silhouette

Pictures like this cut from paper, were very popular in the nineteenth century. Quaker men wore broad-brimmed hats and women and girls wore bonnets.

Friendship Quilt

Friendship quilts were made for special occasions.

Evergreen Farm, Lincoln, Virginia

Winter at Evergreen Farm

Yardley Taylor and his family lived at Evergreen Farm. Fugitives often began their journey in winter under the cover of darkness of long nights.

Evergreen Farm, Lincoln, Virginia

Evergreen Farm Attic Room

Spaces under the eaves of the roof, like this one at Evergreen, were used to hide runaway slaves. A bed or chest pulled in front of this low door would hide it from view.

180

Evergreen Farm Barn

Often runaway slaves hid in the Quakers' barns like this one at Evergreen. The scents of cattle and fodder confused patrol dogs tracking runaways.

Evergreen Farm, Lincoln, Virginia

Evergreen Farm, Lincoln, Virginia

Evergreen Farm Springhouse

Yardley Taylor went often to Philadelphia to meet with the publisher of his maps. He would bring back rare and unusual trees and plants. This bald cypress tree at Evergreen, growing near the springhouse, is more than 150 years old.

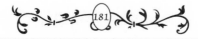

Courtesy, Loudoun Museum, Leesburg, Virginia

Yardley Taylor

Yardley Taylor spoke out about the evils of slavery and was willing to risk arrest to help slaves escape. Mapmaker, horticulturist, abolitionist, social scientist, and more, Yardley Taylor was known as the "Thomas Jefferson of Loudoun County".

Oakdale School, Lincoln, Virginia

Oakdale School

The Quakers of Goose Creek (now called Lincoln), Virginia, built Oakdale School for their children. About 35 children of all ages attended this one-room school.

Free State
Slave State
Territory
general movement

*Map, from THE UNDERGROUND RAILROAD
by Raymond Bial; Houghton Mifflin Company

Underground Railroad Map

The Underground Railroad had many routes north to freedom. After
the Fugitive Slave Act of 1850, freedom often meant Canada.

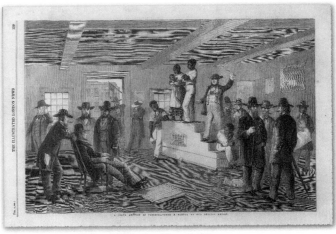

A Slave Auction in Virginia, The Illustrated London News, February 16, 1861

Slave Auction

The slave auctions were places where slaves were bought and sold. Sometimes a family was sold together, but more often than not, family members went to different slave owners.

Chicago Historical Society. After the Sale: Slaves Going South from Richmond 1853; ICHi-31993: Artist: Eyre Crowe

After the Sale

Slave traders strike th deals, money changes han and families are separat forever. The separation family members was one the most brutal aspects slavery.

Pearl's Tag

Slave owners put tags on slaves to prove they were the property of a certain plantation. Here is an example of the kind of tag Pearl might have worn.

Front   Back

A Ride for Liberty–The Fugitive Slaves by Eastman Johnson, ca 1862; Brooklyn Museum of Art

Ride to Liberty

This painting shows a slave family escaping together. It was rare, however, for an entire family to escape at the same time.

Free! by H.L. Stephens, 1863, Courtesy, Library of Congress

"Free!"

Liberty Letters

Now the Lord is Spirit; and where the Spirit of the Lord is, there is Liberty.
2 Corinthians 3:17

Dear Reader:

When I wrote Liberty Letters, I intended to communicate America's journey of freedom and also to illustrate the personal faith journey of girls who made bold choices to help others and in doing so, helped shape the course of history. Through their stories, we learn the facts, customs, lifestyles of days gone by, and so much more.

The girls I wrote about didn't consider themselves part of "history." Few people do. These were ordinary girls going about their lives when challenging times occurred in the communities in which they lived. They discovered integrity, courage, hope, and faith within themselves as they met these challenges with creativity and innovation. American history is steeped with just these kinds of people. These people embody liberty.

I wrote Underground Railroad while looking out over the property of Evergreen Farm. I could almost feel the land speaking to me and saying: "Tell the stories of a thousand Josephs and Pearls and Tookies."

I researched newspaper articles, broadsides, the Goose Creek Meeting records, and other documents to learn as much as I could about Yardley Taylor, Lucretia Mott, Daniel Dangerfield, and others. I read thousands of pages of original slave narratives. I visited Philadelphia and stood where Lucretia Mott preached.

Sarah's Aunt Alice was modeled after Hannah Whitehall Smith, who was raised in a Pennsylvania Quaker home. Hannah Smith was the wife of Robert Pearsall Smith, the Philadelphia publisher of Yardley Taylor's famous Loudoun County map. Her book, The Christian's Secret of a Happy Life, has sold millions of copies over the last one-hundred fifty years. Mrs. Smith believed that a life of faith was an adventure and a partnership of trust with a vital, powerful, loving God who deeply cared about people.

Today we face new and different challenges in our world, but the need for justice, mercy, and faith is just as strong as ever. My prayer is that perhaps you too will trust God with an adventure of your own that can change your world.

Your Friend,

Nancy LeSourd

The Personal Correspondence of Emma Edmonds and Mollie Turner

Assignment: Civil War Spies, 1862

In this book, Emma Edmonds, a Civil War nurse from the North, corresponds with Mollie Turner, a Christian from the South. Mollie is torn by her role in the war, but when a friendship sparks between her and Emma, they each find strength and a greater sense of duty to contribute to the Union's war efforts. Also includes a historic photo section of life during this era.

Hardcover 0-310-70352-2

Available now at your local bookstore!

Zonder**kidz**.

Liberty Letters™

The personal correspondence of
Catherine Clark and *Meredith Lyons*

Pearl Harbor, 1941
Nancy LeSourd

Zonderkidz

The Personal Correspondence of Catherine Clark and Meredith Lyons

Pearl Harbor, 1941

In this book, close friends, Catherine Clark and Meredith Lyons, find strength in their friendship when their fathers are sent to Pearl Harbor during World War II. When Catherine's father, a naval officer, leaves for Pearl Harbor, the rest of the family stays in Washington because of her brother's illness. Of course, the girls are disappointed, especially since Meredith's family has already moved to Honolulu; thus, begins their correspondence. Their friendship proves to be invaluable as they share their stories about their involvement in the war effort through letters. Also includes a historic photo section of life during this era.

Hardcover 0-310-70353-0

Available now at your local bookstore!

Zonderkidz.

We want to hear from you. Please send your comments about this book to us in care of zreview@zondervan.com. Thank you.

Zonder**kidz**®

Grand Rapids, MI 49530
www.zonderkidz.com